THE ZOO OF IMPOSSIBLE ANIMALS

BOOK ONE: INTO THE UNDERZOO

THE ZOO OF
IMPOSSIBLE
ANIMALS

BOOK ONE:
INTO THE UNDERZOO

Rob Crisell

DE PORTOLA PRESS
TEMECULA

De Portola Press
P.O. Box 891821
Temecula, CA 92589

First edition
10 9 8 7 6 5 4 3 2 1 0

ISBN: 978-0692473634

Cover Illustration by Steve Feldman (stevefeldman.com)
Author photograph by Eric Emanuel
Typography and cover design by Caron Andregg, SeaCliff Media Mktg.

*For my wife Monisha and our children Soren and Miranda,
who—despite not being cryptids—are uniquely wonderful,
and for my parents.*

Contents

Cryptid \ ʻkrip-tid \ noun: [from Gk *kryptos:* hidden] A creature whose existence has been suggested by historical or eyewitness accounts, but has never been given scientific credit.

The Four Laws of Cryptozoology

1. Cryptids are experts at hiding.
2. Cryptids vigorously defend their hiding places.
3. People and cryptids don't mix.
4. The cryptid you *don't* see is the most dangerous one of all.

Prologue

It's weird what someone thinks about right before a giant blue tiger tears him into a million pieces.

Jake mostly thought about what a jerk he'd been. Why hadn't he been a better son to his mom? Why hadn't he been nicer to his sister? Why had he pulled so many pranks and gotten kicked out of so many schools? Why did he basically force his family to move from Washington, D.C. to New Mexico?

But at this particular moment, the thought that really nagged at him was: How in the world did he wind up in the cage of a maniacal, blue tiger?

However, there was no more time for regrets. The tiger leaped, its razor-sharp claws catching the morning sunlight.

This was gonna hurt, thought Jake, squeezing his eyes shut.

This was gonna hurt *a lot*.

1

Welcome to the Middle of Nowhere

He would really, really liked to say that all his problems began with an ink monkey named Pablo.

In reality, though, they started with him—Jake Jinks: thirteen-year old underachiever, practical joker, and general misfit. After all, it was definitely his fault that their mother interrupted their reasonably comfortable life in Washington, D.C. to haul his sister Miranda and him across the country to New Mexico. Even if he had wanted to blame everything on Pablo, Miranda would never have let him.

As they sat down in the minivan at the beginning of their cross-country trip, she turned to him, her eyes blood-shot and puffy from crying.

"I am *never* talking to you again, Jake," she said angrily. "That's a promise."

He shrugged. Miranda's threats didn't usually scare him. She got mad at him all the time and got over it within a few hours. Besides, even though she was painfully shy, she was also a know-it-all. He assumed that meant she wouldn't be able to keep her mouth shut for more than a couple minutes, let alone forever.

He was wrong. She turned out to be a lot more determined than he thought. She mostly ignored him the entire 2,989-mile journey to New Mexico. She even directed questions meant for him to their mother, which was super annoying.

But he couldn't really hold it against her. He would have ignored himself if he could have turned off his own thoughts.

Until last month, they'd been living in a townhouse in Washington, D.C. where their mother worked as a physician at a local clinic about five blocks from the Capitol Building. She enjoyed her job, but it kept her busy all the time. His father had disappeared right after Jake was born. Their mother didn't like to talk about it. They sometimes wondered whether she even knew all the details. All she would tell them is that he had been working for the army on a top-secret mission in South America when something went terribly wrong.

Jake didn't remember anything about his father. Neither did Miranda, who had been two years old when he left. They only knew what he looked like because of the photos around the house. Jake was tall like his dad. He stood at least a couple inches taller than most of the boys his age. His dad also had the same mop of dark hair and the same big, goofy smile that people often accused Jake of having.

Jake thought things might have turned out differently if he'd grown up with a dad around. Maybe he wouldn't have felt so out of place in the world the way he sometimes did.

His eighth grade year at Friendship Middle School was typical of his academic career up to that point. He wasn't great at school, unlike his brainy sister. Most of his classes bored him senseless, except for computers and math. He also wasn't into sports. Sometimes the only way he could relate to other kids was by being funny. He enjoyed making people laugh and was pretty good at it.

And that's usually how he got in trouble. It felt like by the end of his first week at every school he'd ever attended, he beaome Enemy Number One.

Last October, for instance, Jake thought it would be funny to put those yellow sticky notes on every square inch of Principal Mora's car. (It took three hours, but was totally worth it.) During winter break, he hacked into the school website and gave every student in school a 4.0 average. Everyone patted him on the back and called him a hero when he got back from vacation.

Except for Principal Mora, who suspended him.

But his all-time favorite prank was his most recent one. He released four hamsters into the teacher's lounge with the numbers one, two, three, and five painted on their fur. The custodians caught all four them within a few hours, but they spent the next three days looking for number four. It turned out that Mrs. Mora has a pathological fear of rodents, even cuddly ones. Under a barrage of threats and pleading, Jake finally admitted that number four didn't actually exist.

In the end, the only reason he didn't flunk out of eighth grade was because the administration really didn't want him to come back the next year.

Jake thought his mother would finally ship him off to that military camp in upstate New York, which she'd been threatening to do for years. Instead, she did something even crazier—something that neither Miranda nor he saw coming at all. The week after school ended, she quit her job at the clinic, said good-bye to her friends, packed all their stuff into a van and a small trailer, and drove them to New Mexico.

At first, this upset him. Then he remembered that he didn't have much of a life in D.C. anyway. How much worse could New Mexico be? he thought. It probably has great Mexican food. How bad could a place be if it has awesome burritos?

Miranda, on the other hand, didn't care about burritos. Their mother's decision sent her on a crying jag for two days straight. Jake knew why. It was her first year at Thomas Jefferson High School and she was the best student in the entire ninth grade. Despite being quiet, she had made several close friends. Of course, all the teachers loved her. She took horseback lessons outside the city on the weekends. She even volunteered at the National Zoo once a month. For a 14-year-old girl, her life was pretty wonderful. Why would anyone want to change it?

So it turned out to be a miserable trip.

Near the end of the fourth day on the road, they saw a weathered wooden sign through their bug-splattered car window. It read:

Welcome to
Ranchita, New Mexico!
Population 1,371
Elevation 2,213 feet

"We're finally here," said their mother, bleary-eyed and exhausted. "Welcome to New Mexico, guys—the Land of Enchantment."

Jake looked out at their new home. It didn't look very enchanting to him. In fact, whatever the opposite of enchanting was, Ranchita was *that*.

The town lay along a two-lane highway that stretched from the edge of a desert on one side to some kind of pine-covered wilderness on the other. Brown hills rose up on either side of the valley with some taller, gray mountains behind them. There were a couple convenience stores, a police station, several churches, and a fire station. He spotted a run-down Mexican restaurant next to an abandoned Burger Barn with weeds growing through cracks in the parking lot. There were big clumps of cactus growing in the vacant lots between the buildings.

Wow, he thought. This place is a total wasteland.

"When did the town get hit by an asteroid?" he asked innocently.

His mom glared at him. "Don't even start with me, young man," she said. "Aunt Jenny and her family lived in Ranchita for years. We're lucky that she just retired to Florida to live with my cousin Sam. And it's only a half hour to my new clinic in Sandoval. So it's fresh-start time for both of you." She narrowed her eyes at Jake. "Especially you, mister."

Miranda peered out at the tall mountains that ringed the valley. "I thought you said New Mexico had lots of culture, Mom. This place is a desert."

"Yeah," agreed Jake. "A desert on Mars."

"Mars doesn't have gas stations," replied their mother. "Anyway, you'll have the whole summer to adjust. You'll get used to it."

They didn't talk again until the van stopped in front of a house that sat at the end of a long dirt road off the main highway. They got out of the car. Jake stretched his arms and looked around.

It was an ancient two-story home with a wooden porch that wrapped all the way around it. Bare wood showed through the peeling paint of the siding, which might have been blue at one time but was now sort of a dirty gray. There was a porch swing to the left of the front door that hung crookedly on rusted chains. Clumps of cactus and spikey weeds as tall as parking meters were everywhere. To the left, there were some wooden corrals that might have held horses or cows at one time. A dead tree had fallen across one section of the fence.

"We've got a lot of cleaning up to do around here," said their mother, surveying the property. "I know we can get this place looking great in no time."

"At least there are no traffic jams," said Jake. "No pollution either. I mean, if you don't count cow poop."

Miranda shot him a look that made his insides twist up like a garden hose. "You're not funny. Let's just go inside, OK?"

As they went into the house, Jake thought about his sister. Miranda could be summed up in two words, he thought. Perfectly annoying. That is, she was perfect *and* annoying. She was fourteen years old, with brown eyes and straight brown hair that fell over her shoulders. She was tall for her age, which often made her feel awkward around other kids. She read obsessively and had *way* too many opinions about everything, even though she only seemed to share them with him and their mother. She often seemed to have no sense of humor at all. She tried to be polite, never got in trouble, always got A's, and had the vocabulary of an English teacher. In fact, in some ways, she was his opposite. When people compared him to Miranda, he never came out looking good.

They opened the front door and went inside. Their mother

turned on the lights. The main room had loads of antiques. They saw a red velour couch, dainty coffee tables, a fancy wood dining table, and lots and lots of lace doilies

Judging by the interior decoration, thought Jake, Aunt Jenny must be about 150 years old.

They pulled open all the dusty blinds and dark, olive-green drapes. Miranda opened up the doors to the back porch to let in some fresh air. Jake checked the faucet in the kitchen to make sure there was running water. Then they went up the creaky wooden stairs to look at the bedrooms. Miranda chose the room next to the master bedroom. It had high ceilings with faded flower wallpaper and a window seat with a big cushion with pictures of flowers on it. A queen-sized bed sat in the middle of the room with about an inch of dust on it.

He went into a smaller room near the top of the stairs. It had single bed in it with a small oak desk tucked in the corner. Somebody might have used it as an office once. It smelled stuffy and old, like everything else in the house. He opened the blinds and peered out at the front yard. A truck drove up the long dirt road to their house. It stopped by the front door and three men wearing blue uniforms climbed out.

"Hey, guys!" yelled their mother from downstairs. "The movers are here with the rest of our stuff. Go out back and check out the rest of the property. I'll yell for you when I need you."

So while their mother supervised the movers, Jake and Miranda cautiously walked onto the back porch and down the steps into the yard.

2

A Furry Trespasser

From the porch, Miranda and Jake gazed out over the huge meadow of yellow grass, rock, and dirt that was their backyard. It was as hot and dry as a sauna outside. Yellowing pines swayed gently in the breeze. The cloudless sky was a brilliant blue above the surrounding hills, which looked rocky and gray in the distance. Jake sighed so loudly it sounded more like a groan. It was the first Monday of summer vacation and they were 3,000 miles from where they grew up, with no friends and no idea what they were going to do for the rest of the summer.

"I wonder if there are any good horse trails around here," said Miranda. "Maybe there's a ranch or something nearby. Did you see anything cool when we were in town?"

He tried to stop himself from rolling his eyes at her attempt at enthusiasm. No success.

"No, I didn't see a horse ranch," he said, his voice dripping with sarcasm. "I also didn't see a Starbuck's, a movie theater, or Disneyland. Maybe all that stuff is on another street."

She glared at him. "I'm *so sorry* for my good attitude. Did you ever think about how *I* feel? I was going to spend two weeks at Breezeway Farms Riding Academy. Now I'm hanging out the whole summer with the Class Clown of the Year in a desert."

Ouch, he thought. That hurts. "There was never an official election," he mumbled. "Let's just go see how big this place is."

They were both sweating by the time they reached a long stretch of wooden fence. On the other side of it, a stream crawled along the base of the mountain toward a forest of pine trees in the distance.

"I guess this is where the property ends," said Miranda.

"I guess so," he replied. "I wonder how far this fence runs along the stream."

"Why do you care?" she asked scornfully. "You said this place is a wasteland, right?"

He wiped the sweat from his brow with the back of his hand. It was one thing for his sister to ignore him during the car trip from D.C., he thought. But he'd go crazy if she stayed angry at him for the whole summer.

"Look, Miranda," he said. "I already apologized about a thousand times. *I* didn't want to move here. If you want to blame somebody, blame Mom. You act like it's my fault."

"It *is* your fault!" she said, her eyes beginning to water. "How can somebody get in so much trouble all the time? We moved here because of *you* and you know it. You never think of anyone but yourself."

"I can't help it if nobody at Friendship could take a joke," he said. "Look—if I knew Mom was going to freak out and move us to New Mexico, I would have tried a lot harder. Probably."

She sighed. "Whatever," she said. "I just don't know how I'm ever going to get used to this place. It's so awful." She looked around. "I have a weird feeling we're being watched."

"Seriously?" he asked.

"Look," she said, pointing. "Over there."

Sitting on a wooden fence post about ten yards away, a tiny creature stared at them with obvious curiosity. It had silky, golden, reddish-brown hair and a long tail that seemed to curl around itself. Two tufts of white hair jutted out from either side of its head in neat triangles. It had a snub nose that it twitched as it smelled them. But the most striking thing about the animal was its eyes, which resembled two black almonds set against a bright blue mask. It was as if the monkey had emptied a tube of neon-blue mascara on its face.

"Oh, wow," Jake said. "It's some kind of mutant squirrel. Do you think somebody spray painted its face?"

"That can't be a squirrel," she replied. "I think it's a monkey. Don't you see its tail? Look at its tiny paws. And that blue face!" Her eyes softened and she smiled. "Maybe it's hungry. Do you have something we could feed it?"

He rummaged through his pants pockets. He pulled out a completely melted candy bar, about twenty gum wrappers, a pen, three rubber bands, and some lint.

Miranda made a disgusted face. "Gross. He's not going to eat any of that. What we need is—"

But before she could finish, the little monkey scrambled down the fence post and scurried across the dry grass toward them. The monkey seemed barely to touch the ground as it walked. It tilted its head and edged nearer until it sat only a few feet away.

Jake knelt down and carefully laid the items from his pocket onto the grass. He noticed that the monkey wore a collar with a gold emblem on it.

"Look," he whispered. "It has a nametag. It must be somebody's pet."

The golden monkey studied the objects on the ground. It quickly snatched up the pen, ran back to the fence, and scooted up the post. Then to their amazement, it snapped the pen in half and began sucking out the ink as if it were a straw.

Miranda's eyes widened in alarm. "What is it doing?"

He blinked, not believing his eyes. "I think it's eating the ink," he said.

"That can't be good," she said. "I'll get it away from him."

She took a short, cautious step toward the fence.

And the monkey vanished. One second it was on a post chewing a pen and the next second it was gone.

Miranda gasped. "What happened? Where did it go?"

"He's *fast!*" exclaimed Jake. He bent down to pick up his stuff from the grass. "Oh, well. He was a little weirdo anyway. I mean, what kind of animal eats ink? He probably has rabies."

"He does *not* have rabies," she said defensively. "You would know that if you watched every episode of *Animal Planet* like I have."

"Whatever," he said.

His sister adored animals. She fell in love with every horse she ever rode. She was constantly asking their mom for a dog, even though she was allergic to them. There wasn't a nature program on television that she hadn't seen at least once. A mysterious, blue-faced monkey was right up her alley.

"I wonder who he belongs to," she said. "Do you think there's an address or phone number on his tag?"

"Probably," said Jake, shrugging. "But we could never catch him anyway. You saw how quick he ran away. If I were you, I'd forget about it."

But he knew his sister wouldn't be able to forget the trespassing monkey.

To his surprise, he realized he wouldn't either.

3

Return of the Ink Monkey

The next morning as Jake and Miranda ate their scrambled eggs and bacon in the kitchen, their mother made an announcement.

"I've decided that this will be the summer of relaxation and reevaluation," she said in an upbeat voice. "I think a little one-on-one time with each other will be good for both of you."

"Relaxing and reevaluating?" said Jake incredulously. "I'm horrible at both those things."

"You'll be fine," she said. "Anyway, until I get a handle on the clinic, that's how it has to be. I'll be working some long days and nights for a while."

"Can I at least have a cell phone?" asked Miranda.

She shook her head. "No phones until you're fifteen. You know the rule. When you start school in the fall I'll get you one."

Worst rule ever, thought Jake bitterly.

"Call me on the home phone if there's an emergency," said their mother, giving them each a hug. "And *please* try to get out of the house a little. I know it's hot, but I don't want your brains to turn into pudding."

She walked out the front door, got into the minivan, and drove down the dirt road to the highway.

When she was gone, Miranda gazed thoughtfully out the window. "If we go back to the place by the fence, do you think that monkey would show up again?" she wondered. "We could bring it an apple or something this time."

Jake carried his empty plate to the sink. "I doubt it. He probably got nabbed by a hawk or a coyote or something. I bet a rabbit could take him down."

She scowled at him. "I'm immune to your humor, remember? Somebody has to be the mature one." She got up from the table. "I'm going outside to do my calligraphy."

"Have fun with that, grump," he said.

In his opinion, calligraphy had to be the most boring hobby ever invented. It basically consisted of using a fancy pen to make pretty-looking words in cursive writing. If you messed up even one letter, you had to do the whole page over again. He'd tried it once two years before. All he managed to do was to stain his fingers black for a week. But calligraphy was endlessly fun for a quiet, humorless nerd like his sister.

While Miranda sat writing at the decaying wicker table on the back porch, he lay down on the red couch in the living room. He listened to music on his iPod and leafed through one of Aunt Jenny's coffee table books about cake decorating. After a while, he grabbed an apple and a bag of chips and went outside by Miranda to play Castleopolis. As he sat down in one of the lawn chairs, he heard Miranda noisily clear her throat. He looked up.

On the top step of the porch sat the same small, golden monkey with the blue face they'd seen the day before. It stared at them with black, oval eyes, his tail twitching like a trained cobra. The golden tag on its collar glinted brightly in the morning sun.

"Don't you have anything better to do, little guy?" Jake asked. "There's nothing to see here but a colossal train wreck of boredom."

"Shh!" said Miranda. "You're going to scare him. Look at him—he's really jumpy."

The monkey *did* look especially nervous this morning, Jake thought. It kept hopping two inches to one side, then the other.

"I'll give him the rest of my apple," he said. "I bet he likes fruit."

Miranda nodded. "Try it."

He took his partially eaten apple and reached out as far as he could. He placed it a few feet away from the monkey. The animal came forward slowly, sniffed at it, and then sat back on its haunches, staring up at them impatiently.

"I guess he doesn't like apples," he said. "What the heck does he want then?"

Miranda's eyes brightened. "I have an idea. I'm going to give him my ink bottle.

Jake's eyebrows arched warily. "What are you trying to do? Kill him? Just because he chewed on that pen yesterday doesn't mean he wants a gallon of ink."

"It's hardly a gallon," she said as she picked up the bottle and placed it carefully next to the apple. "Trust me. I think he wants some ink."

The monkey glanced at the bottle curiously with its dark almond-shaped eyes. He hopped over to it, picking it up with both tiny, golden paws. Its eyes seemed to grow wider. It flicked out a blue tongue to lick the mouth of the bottle. Then it flipped the entire thing upside into its mouth and gulped it down.

Oh, no, thought Jake. The monkey's crazy! And we just helped it poison itself.

When it finished drinking all the ink from the bottle, the monkey dropped it next to the apple and sat back on its tiny haunches. It wrapped its tail around itself. It closed its eyes and began making a purring sound.

"OK, *that's* weird," said Jake. "Now what are we supposed to do?"

"He looks calmer now," she said. "I'm going to try to pick him up."

She gently scooped up the animal in her hands. To Jake's surprise, the monkey didn't try to run away. In fact, it acted like it had expected to be picked up. It opened its black eyes sleepily and blinked a few times before shutting them again.

"What does he feel like?" asked Jake, eyeing the monkey curiously.

"Like the softest kitten you've ever held times ten," she said. She held out the monkey. "See for yourself."

"Are you sure?" he asked. "Maybe he's got a thing against Class Clowns of the Year."

"Probably." She grinned. "But there's only one way to find out."

Jake stretched out his arms as she handed him the golden monkey. When the animal saw him reach for him, he squeaked and retreated to Miranda's shoulder, wrapping its tail gently around her neck.

"Hey!" exclaimed Jake. "I'd be insulted if you weren't so darn cute. I guess I'll have to find my own bottle of ink to bribe him into letting me hold him."

Miranda laughed. "Don't take it personally, Jake," she said. "He probably can tell you're not much of an animal lover."

He grunted. "Well, he's right about that." He leaned over and stroked the monkey on his head, which it didn't seem to mind. "Now let's see who you belong to." He gently grasped the gold tag on the monkey's collar. "It says: 'My name is Pablo. *Simianus atramenta.*'" He turned over the back of the tag. "'Please return me to One Hidden Valley Road, Ranchita, NM.' That's it. No phone number or email."

Miranda reached up and carefully removed the monkey from her shoulder, cradling it in her arms. "The Latin should tell us what kind of animal he is," she explained. "OK, Pablo, let's find out what you are."

They walked into the house and sat down at the kitchen table in front of the laptop. The golden monkey immediately climbed down from Miranda's shoulder and scrambled over to the center island in the kitchen. He began exploring as if he owned the place.

"You better keep an eye on him," said Jake. "I'll find out where Hidden Valley Road is. It can't be too far away if it's in Ranchita." A dozen keystrokes later, the screen showed a map of the entire area. "Hidden Valley is only a couple miles east of us." He pointed to the red arrow on the screen. "You can only get there by this private road. It's at the end of the dirt road our house is on, but instead of taking a left you keep going toward the mountains."

Pablo continued to inspect the kitchen, occasionally peeking inside jars or opening drawers. Suddenly, they heard a splash as the monkey fell into the sink filled with soapy water and dishes from breakfast.

"Oops," said Miranda, running over to the sink. "You have to be more careful, Pablo." She pulled him gently out of the water. He now bore a striking resemblance to a drenched rat wearing bright blue goggles. She found a towel and gently dried him off.

Jake typed in *simianus atramenta* in the search engine. No hits. He tried again on a different site, and then another. He leaned back in the chair. "Weird. According to the internet, there's no such thing as a *simianus atramenta.*"

Miranda came over to the computer with Pablo wrapped in a white towel like a baby. "Try typing in each word separately."

Jake typed in *simianus*. Hits about monkeys, gorillas, and apes filled the screen. "OK. *Simianus* is the Latin name for 'monkey'. That makes sense." He typed in *atramenta*.

"*Atramenta* is Latin for ink," said Miranda, reading over his shoulder. "So Pablo must be an ink monkey."

Jake frowned. "I guess that explains what he just ate for breakfast. But I've never heard of an ink monkey. Have you?"

She shook her head. "Nope. Keep looking."

He typed in *ink monkey* and scrolled through the first three pages of entries. There were several tattoo parlors and a print shop in Chicago that went by the name, but no animals. "I'm sure somebody is just trying to be funny. I can appreciate that."

"He sort of resembles a golden snub-nosed monkey to me," said Miranda, as Pablo squirmed out of his towel and continued his inspection of the kitchen. "I think they're from China. It's really unusual for monkeys to have that blue coloration around their eyes."

Jake typed in *golden monkey*. Several pictures of adorable, round-eyed primates appeared on screen. Golden snub-nose monkeys resembled Pablo a little, but they were much bigger. He also doubted that normal golden monkeys ate ink.

They looked up. Pablo sat near the bay window holding one of their mother's expensive silver pens in its tiny paws.

"Pablo, no!" shouted Miranda. "Don't—"

It was too late. The monkey broke the pen in two like a Pixie Stick and began sucking out the ink.

"This guy's got a serious inking problem," said Jake, grinning. "Get it? Anyway, at least we have the address of his owner. We can just take him to his house and give him back."

Miranda's expression grew sad. "Do we *have* to do it today? Let's keep him for a few days."

Jake shook his head. "He might get cabin fever and take off again. Or he'll croak from all that ink he's eating. I think we should return him today. We have plenty of time. Mom won't be home until tonight."

She sighed. "I guess you're right. But how are we going to get there? It's too far to walk."

"We can take our bikes," he said. "You can put Pablo in a backpack with a few pens and we'll ride out to Hidden Valley Road. I bet we can get there and back in a few hours."

He could see she really didn't want to return an animal as cute as Pablo. With her beloved white pony Handyman out of the picture, this was a new creature she could take care of.

"I don't know," she said doubtfully. "Mom will kill us if she finds out we went so far away."

"You worry too much, sis," he said. "As the cooler, more daring sibling in this family, I hereby give you permission to relax. Come on! You might have fun for once."

She rolled her eyes. "Like I'm going to take advice from my juvenile-delinquent little brother." She paused, thinking about it. "Oh, why not? Let's do it!"

4

A Secret Zoo

With Pablo clinging contentedly to her shoulder, Miranda went to fix sandwiches for their trip. By the time Jake took the bikes out of the garage and put air in the tires, she was standing on the front porch. The golden monkey's head peeked out of her backpack, his blue face highlighting his serene black eyes.

"I brought him some pens to chew on," she said. "He won't enjoy them as much as my organic calligraphy ink, but they'll hold him until we get there."

"Good idea," he replied. "I've got the bikes. Let's go."

After only ten minutes of pedaling down the long dirt road from their house, Jake already felt his shirt damp on his back. Hot gusts of wind stirred up the dust, forcing them to grip the handles of their bikes more tightly. They took a right turn at the end of their road and headed west. Low fences of rusted barbed wire enclosed huge expanses of windswept dirt and dead grass on either side of them.

After a half hour, the road ended at a massive gate that stood at the mouth of a steep canyon. The gate was solid steel. It rose eight feet high with tall brick columns on either side. A tall wire fence stretched away from it on both sides. Signs showed stick figures being zapped by electricity.

A bronze placard on one of the pylons read:

PRIVATE – Z.I.A. Inc.
Absolutely no visitors allowed.
Trespassers will be prosecuted.
Turn around now!

They lay their bikes down at the edge of the road and walked over to the gate. Two security cameras were mounted on top of the gate. To their left, they saw a panel with buttons on it.

Miranda eyed the gate nervously. "I don't think they get many visitors. Maybe we should head back."

"No way," said Jake. "We've got an ink monkey to deliver. Besides, with a gate this big, can you imagine how awesome this guy's house is? I want to see it."

There were no numbers or words on the panel to show what any of the buttons meant. He pressed a few of them at random. Nothing happened.

"Hello? Anybody home?" he asked.

Suddenly, a voice boomed from what seemed like fifty loud speakers. "YOU ARE ON PRIVATE PROPERTY!" They winced and covered their ears as Pablo ducked back inside the backpack. "LEAVE THE PREMISES IMMEDIATELY OR WE WILL NOTIFY THE POLICE!"

Notify the police? thought Jake. They were trying to bring back this guy's lost pet and he was threatening to have them arrested? What a total jerk.

Without thinking, he picked up a rock and hurled it at one of the cameras. It missed by two feet, but it made him feel a little better.

"We have your stupid monkey!" he shouted, pointing to Miranda's backpack. "Your M-O-N-K-E-Y." He rocked back and forth like an ape in a Hollywood movie. He beat his chest, scratched his armpits, and made a few loud squeeks.

"That's not helping, Jake," said Miranda. She took off her backpack and unzipped it slightly. Pablo stuck out his head and peeped around. "See?" she said, looking up at the camera. "We found Pablo, your ink monkey."

It was silent for a few seconds. "What did you call the animal?" asked the voice.

"Ink monkey!" they shouted in unison.

Silence again. "Someone will meet you shortly," said the voice at last. "Don't move."

Still no "please" or "thank you," thought Jake. At least they didn't threaten to call the cops this time.

After five minutes, they heard a humming sound and the gate began to open. Through the gap they saw the road continuing deep into the canyon. They also saw a small vehicle driving toward them at high speed—a kind of fancy black golf cart with knobby, off-road wheels. The car halted directly in front of them and a man climbed out of it. It was the tallest person they'd ever seen. He stood well over seven feet tall, with skin the color of onyx. He wore a black robe with bright rainbow-colored fabric woven into it. The kind of thing an African king might wear on special occasions, thought Jake. On top of the man's head sat a boxy cap that matched the robe. He smiled broadly, signaling with his hand for them to join him in the cart.

Jake didn't know how he felt about driving anywhere with the man in the colorful robe. "We found your monkey." He pointed at Miranda's backpack. "We'll just give him to you and leave. It's obvious that you're not used to company."

The man smiled again, gesturing with his massive hand for them to join him. Jake glanced nervously at Miranda.

"Don't you want to take him?" she asked, stepping forward. She held out the backpack to him. "We don't want to be a bother or anything."

The man cupped his hands as if he were holding something in them. Then he pointed to Pablo, who stared at him warily from Miranda's backpack. He pretended to place an object in his hands and then waved his hands, as if to indicate that the object had disappeared.

"I'm horrible at charades," mumbled Jake. "What are you, uh, *not* talking about?"

"Oh, I get it!" exclaimed Miranda. "You're saying that Pablo will run away if we take him out of the bag. Right?"

The man nodded and smiled again, giving her a thumb's up sign.

Miranda turned to Jake. "It wouldn't hurt to see his house for a few minutes. Maybe he's got some other rare animals. I think it will be OK."

Jake could think of about a hundred reasons why this was a bad idea. At the same time, despite being almost as tall as a basketball hoop, the man in the cart seemed to be trustworthy. He shrugged. "Fine with me."

"We'll go with you and drop Pablo off in his cage or whatever," explained Miranda. "But then we have to get back to our house before our mom calls the cops. Because she knows we're here. Right, Jake?

"Right," he replied quickly. "Of course. It would have been

stupid and reckless *not* to tell her."

They got into the cart. Miranda removed the pack and placed it on her lap. Pablo peeped out of it, eyeing the man behind the wheel. As they drove away, the huge gate closed slowly behind them.

If this guy wanted to lock them up in his house, thought Jake, their mother wouldn't even know where they went. But it turned out he wasn't taking them to a house at all.

He was taking them to a *zoo*.

5

Welcome to the Z.I.A.

It didn't take brilliant powers of observation for Jake to realize that the enormous man in the colorful outfit was driving them to a zoo. He just read the wooden placard hanging on the gate:

ZOO OF IMPOSSIBLE ANIMALS
Cryptid Research, Detection & Control
No photography allowed!
Remember: Loose lips = One-way Trips

The Zoo of Impossible Animals? What the heck did *that* mean? Was a cryptid an impossible animal? And why did they need detecting and controlling? His excitement was dampened a bit by the thought that they might be tossed to lions or thrown in a piranha tank.

Eventually, the road went around a bend and down a long, steep hill. They emerged into a small valley nestled among the rock-encrusted mountains. As they drove, Jake saw several brown wooden buildings on stilts, like ones he'd seen in books about Africa.

The vehicle stopped in front of one of the buildings. There were more structures further into the valley about two hundred yards away. In the midst of them, a steel tower rose up one hundred feet into the air. At the top of the tower sat a large structure made entirely of tinted glass.

"What *is* that?" asked Miranda, her eyes widening. "Is it some kind of military base? It couldn't be somebody's house, could it?"

"I have no idea," he said. "If it's a house, the person who lives there has really strange taste in architecture."

They followed the huge man up the steps into the building. Inside, at an elegant desk of polished wood with inlaid panels of ebony, sat a pale man in his forties. He had a thin, blond mustache, light-colored hair, and bright blue eyes behind reading glasses. He wore a neatly pressed khaki uniform. His name tag read: *Professor Markus Becker, Director, Z.I.A., Inc.*

He seemed like an accountant pretending to be a lion tamer, thought Jake. Or maybe the other way around.

Next to the professor stood a short, bald Asian man with such a nasty scowl that Jake wondered if he'd ever smiled in his life. He scanned his name tag: *Alan Feng, Assistant Director, Z.I.A., Inc.* The Asian man spoke first.

"What are *they* doing here, Dembi?" he asked their driver, clearly annoyed. "Did they climb the gate? Or is that hole in the fence by Elephant Ridge still not repaired?"

The man named Dembi frowned and shook his head. He gestured at Miranda, who turned slightly to reveal Pablo, who poked his head out of the backpack. The monkey took one look at Feng, made a loud squeak, and disappeared back into the pack.

"Do calm down, Alan," said Professor Becker. He smiled at them kindly, removing his glasses. He spoke with a slight

European accent. German maybe, thought Jake. "Dembi obviously allowed these two young people into the zoo because they managed to catch the ever-elusive Pablo." He nodded at Jake and Miranda. "Capturing an ink monkey is no easy task. They are blindingly fast and clever. I am *very* impressed."

Feng's sour expression showed he didn't share his boss's assessment. "Another escaped cryptid! That's the fourth one this month. I'm calling Bolo. He needs be made aware of this immediately." He took a cell phone from his belt and pressed a button. "Bolo? You're needed in Professor Becker's office. Another cryptid escaped from its enclosure." He paused, scowling. "How should *I* know? Just hurry up." He ended his call and returned his attention to Jake and Miranda. "So what do you want? A reward, I suppose?"

Jake felt himself losing his temper. First, somebody threatens to call the police on them outside the gate. Now this jerk gives them a ridiculously hard time for no reason.

"We don't want a reward," Jake said, his voice rising. "All we wanted to do was to give you back your monkey. Next time, we'll take him to the pound. By the way, he ate every pen in our house, so he might barf on your shoes later. I *hope* he does anyway."

Feng glared at Jake, his face turning red. He opened his mouth to say something, but Professor Becker stood up from his desk. He held his hand up, as if warning Feng to be quiet. He was thin and very tall, at least half a half-foot taller than Jake. His khaki uniform clung to him like a scarecrow. He opened a drawer in his desk and removed a small bottle of black ink from it. Pablo, who had poked his head out of the backpack again, wiggled out of the pack and jumped onto the desk. Before the monkey could grab the bottle of ink, the man scooped him up in one quick motion and held him firmly.

"You'll have to forgive Mr. Feng," said Professor Becker. "Several of the zoo's prized specimens have gone missing in recent weeks and we're all under quite a bit of stress. Believe me—we are very grateful to you for returning Pablo to us." He shot Feng a cold glance that made Jake think that someone was getting chewed out later.

Suddenly, the office door opened and a man stepped into the room. He looked almost as tall as Professor Becker but was much more muscular, with a neck as thick as a tree stump. He had deeply tanned skin and his head was shaved into a crew cut. He had a jagged scar that ran from the top of his forehead through his left eyebrow all the way down his cheek to his chin. There were tattoos on his neck and arms, including one that showed a black cobra about to strike. The man studied Jake and Miranda for a moment through dark, expressionless eyes.

"Howdy," he said, grinning at them in a friendly way. He had a thick southern accent that made him sound like an old-fashioned cowboy. "Good to see some fresh faces 'round here." He turned to the Asian man. "What's goin' on, Alan? I got stuff to do."

"What you've got is a lot of nerve," sputtered Feng. "Yet another cryptid escaped and you didn't even notice. You're supposed to be our new head of security!"

"Really, Alan, you must relax," interrupted Professor Becker. "Mr. Young, these children did us the great favor of returning one of our ink monkeys. Apparently, it escaped from its enclosure within the past week. Would you know anything about that?"

"No clue," he replied in a low and rumbling drawl, as if he hadn't had any water for a week. "It ain't my job to monkey-proof the perimeter. If you got a hole in a cage, get one of your keepers to take care of it. I got bigger fish to fry." He turned around to leave.

"That's it?" fumed Feng. "Aren't you even going to put the cryptid back in its pen?"

"Do it yourself," said the tattooed man, heading for door. "I'm heading back to the command center. I have to finish up the cyber-security program for Cazador. Fell free *not* to call me again, Alan."

"Would you mind if I accompany you, Mr. Young?" asked Becker, handing Pablo and the bottle of ink to Dembi. "I'm eager to hear about your progress with the new security protocols."

The tattooed man shrugged. "Suit yourself."

The two men strode out of the office, leaving Dembi, Feng, Miranda, and Jake standing together in an awkward silence.

Well, maybe not Dembi, thought Jake. Silence seemed to be his thing.

Feng glared at Jake and Miranda. "The professor is too kind sometimes. If it were up to me, you'd both be on your way to the Ranchita jail."

"On what charge?" asked Miranda sarcastically. "Rescuing an ink monkey without a license?"

Feng ignored her. "Escort these children directly to the gate," he told Dembi. "Then stuff that ink-eating rat back into his pen."

As Jake followed Dembi out of the office, he felt so angry

that his hands were shaking. To his surprise, he noticed that Dembi seemed upset as well. He frowned as he drove away from the buildings, carefully handing Pablo to Miranda. Then he flashed them a mischievous grin as he took a sharp right down the hill toward the tower and the other buildings.

I guess we're not going directly to the gate after all, thought Jake.

They zipped down the hill toward a couple dozen small structures arranged around meticulous gardens and bubbling water fountains. Beyond them, a lake that seemed to occupy half the valley shimmered in the late morning sun. Neat gravel paths crisscrossed the zoo. There were at least a dozen workers in khaki uniforms raking the paths, carrying buckets, pushing wheelbarrows, and doing other jobs. Most buildings were connected to open enclosures that stretched behind them like enormous backyards. In one of them, Jake saw a tall white bird preening itself. In another, he saw a few creatures that resembled wrinkled, black pigs. They glimpsed flashes of movement and color inside the other structures.

"This place is amazing," said Miranda in awe. "It must be the largest private zoo in the world."

"I guess so," replied Jake. "A private zoo filled with impossible animals. Whatever those are."

As they rode through the compound, they passed beneath the tower. It had an elevator shaft running up from the ground to the glass building. There were antennae and satellite dishes on top of it. The cart finally stopped in front of one of the smaller cages. Dembi turned to Miranda, smiled, and held out his hands.

"Oh, right," she said. As she handed Pablo to him, the monkey gazed at her with its gentle oval eyes. The blue coloring on its face made him seem sad. "Don't worry, little guy. You're home now."

Dembi motioned for them to follow him. They left the cart and walked with him to Pablo's cage. He punched a few numbers on a keypad next to the glass wall and the door opened. He had them wait as he ducked inside. Through the window, they saw him place Pablo inside the pen. The monkey scurried off to join three other golden clumps of fur huddled under some trees by a small stream.

A great big ink monkey family reunion, thought Jake.

Miranda pointed at the small sign on the cage. "'*Simianus atramenta*. Ink Monkey. Yunnan Province, China.' We were right, Jake!"

"Yep," said Jake. "Too bad ink monkeys don't exist, at least according to the internet."

When Dembi returned, they got back in the cart and drove away. Miranda's eyes began to water. Jake patted her on the back. "Don't be sad, sis," he said. "Pablo's with his buddies now. He probably gets to drink a gallon of ink a day."

"I guess you're right," she said, sighing. She pointed up at the glass house on top of the tower. "Who is that?"

Jake craned his head to look up at the tower. An old man wearing an elegant white suit, a black tie, and a wide-brimmed straw hat peered down at them from one of the balconies. He had a long, white beard and shoulder-length silver hair. He held an oversized black cane. He reminded Jake of a wizard from the movies.

"Who is that man, Mr. Dembi?" asked Miranda, gesturing at the tower.

He glanced up toward the tower, smiled, and gently shook his head.

That would Dembi-speak for 'none of your business', thought Jake.

Maybe Dembi regretted taking them to drop off the monkey, especially if the old man was his boss. Either way, their brief tour of the Z.I.A. was over.

6

Dr. Cazador, Man of Mystery

n the two days following their visit to the Z.I.A., Jake kept himself busy by playing video games and thinking of ways to get even with Alan Feng. Miranda, on the other hand, became obsessed with researching the few animals whose names she'd seen during their visit. Jake had to admit that he felt curious, too. Mostly, he was happy that she forgot she was supposed to be mad at him.

"Come over here, Jake," she yelled from the kitchen. "I found a website about squonks. They're the most ridiculous animals. You won't believe what they can do."

"You're right," he said. "I *won't* believe it." He got up and joined her in the kitchen. She sat in front of the laptop, her eyes glued to the screen. "Let me guess. They can burp their ABCs, breathe fire, and live for years on a Twinkie and a teaspoon of water."

He was giving her a hard time, of course. However, a few of the creatures she'd found were almost as bizarre.

"No burping or Twinkies," she replied. "I think you're just hungry. I searched the entire morning and this is the only description of squonks that I could find. It's yet another creature that supposedly doesn't exist—an undiscovered animal."

She was looking at a website called "Creatures of the Mist."

It featured lots of poorly drawn pictures of bizarre animals. He read the passage aloud:

> "The squonk (*Lacrimacorpus dissolvens*) is a legendary creature that lives in the forests of northern Pennsylvania. Legends of squonks originated in the late nineteenth century at the height of the timber industry. Eyewitnesses who have seen the beast report that its skin is ill-fitting and covered with warts and other blemishes. This causes it to hide from plain sight and spend much of its time weeping. Hunters attempting to catch squonks have said that the creature is capable of evading capture by dissolving into a pool of tears and bubbles."

Jake rolled his eyes. "Tears and bubbles?" he said. "Squonks sound even sillier than that bird with one leg that can tell when it's going to rain. You know—the ding dong."

"It's called a shang yang," she said huffily. "Look, I don't trust these descriptions, either. I mean, the only websites with information are sketchy ones like this one. But I saw signs for these animals in front of the enclosures. Why would anyone make signs for animals if they aren't there?"

He shrugged. "I don't know," he said. "Maybe this Professor Becker guy is crazy. He might find a mutant seagull, throw it in a cage, and call it a bing bang."

"A *shang yang,* you dork!" she said, clearly fed up with his jokes. "And I keep telling you, I don't think Feng and Becker are the owners of the Z.I.A. Remember that man with the tattoos and that nasty scar? He mentioned someone named Cazador. I think *he's* the owner."

Jake wanted to ask her when she had become an expert on zoo management structure. Instead, he grabbed an apple from the basket on the counter. Once his sister became obsessed with a subject, she was like a rocket ship blasting into space. At some point, there were only two choices: get on board or get out of the way.

"And I suppose you think this Cazador is the old guy in the tower?" he asked, taking a bite of the apple.

"I think so," she said eagerly. "His full name is Dr. Jorge Isidoro de San Luis Cazador. There's not much information about him online, but I guess he's been collecting exotic animals most of his life. He calls them *cryptids*—animals that have been hinted at in historical records, but whose existence has never been confirmed by science. Some people call them the beasts that hide from man."

"Well, if you found it on the Internet, it *must* be true," said Jake sarcastically. "Look, Miranda, the guy's probably off his rocker. Also, his name is way too long. Two or three names should be enough for anybody."

"That's not the point. Anyway, people just call him Cazador."

He grinned. "Wait a second!" he said. "You want to go back there, don't you? You're hoping that this Cazador guy will take you on a personal tour of his whacky zoo."

She looked up from the laptop and smiled sheepishly. "OK, maybe I do. Do you think we could sneak in? No offense, but you're the expert in mischief and mayhem."

He knew he should be offended, but he wasn't. He *was* kind of an expert. And a zoo full of bizarre, possibly mythological animals was pretty irresistible. The thought of going back to the Z.I.A. had crossed his mind more than once in the last two days. Of course, he didn't want Miranda to know that.

"Let me get this straight," he began slowly. "You want us to break into the zoo, see as many cool animals as we can before we get thrown out or shot, and—if possible—meet the old man who lives in the tower who may or may not be the owner?"

She swallowed hard. "Somebody might shoot us? Why would they do *that?*"

"You never know," he replied casually, as if he got shot at all the time. "That Feng guy looks mean enough to do it. And what are we supposed to tell Mom? 'Hi, Mom. We're going to break into a zoo with a bunch of weird animals in it and at least one zoo keeper who hates our guts. See you soon!'"

"We don't have to tell her," she said quickly. "Not yet, anyway. Also, Cazador isn't going to shoot a couple kids. It's not his style."

He frowned. "What the heck do you know about his *style?*"

"Judging from the articles I've been reading, he's an amazing man," she said. "He's a billionaire, inventor, explorer, and cryptozoologist. He's not going to let his employees shoot us."

"You're not even sure that guy we saw in the glass house is Cazador," he said. "He could be the janitor."

She gave him a look. "In a white, three-piece suit and that fancy walking stick? Really?"

Jake thought about it. "A well-paid janitor?"

"No, I don't think so. Look at this."

She pressed a few buttons on the keyboard. An article appeared on the screen from a British online magazine called *Zoology Today.* The headline read: "Jorge Cazador—Genius or Fraud?" After a few sentences, it was clear that William T. Boomswanger, the author of the article, knew the answer:

Born in Buenos Aires and raised in London, eccentric entrepreneur and amateur zoologist Dr. Jorge Isidoro de San Luis Cazador is a riddle, wrapped in a mystery, hidden inside a heavily fortified, secret zoo. In the end, however, he's little more than a joke.

Doctor Cazador made his fortune in the United States in the 1960s and 1970s. Some of his more famous inventions include AstroTurf, aluminum can pull-tabs, and the staple remover. He took the money he earned from these inventions and invested in some of the biggest companies of the modern era: Microsoft, Coca-Cola, Apple, and others. A billionaire at age thirty five, Cazador spent the next three decades studying and collecting exotic animals.

However, he wasn't content with "normal" exotics. As I discovered when I interviewed the reclusive Cazador earlier this year, the eccentric amateur zoologist is solely interested in what he calls "cryptozoology." The field of cryptozoology purports to study creatures and plants whose existence is unrecognized by scientific consensus or deemed as highly unlikely, even semi-mythical.

Cazador informed me that he has spent years traveling the world in search of allegedly extinct, extremely rare, and even outright mythical animals. He and his colleagues bring specimens to his secret compound somewhere in the southwest called the Zoo of Impossible Animals.

He declined to discuss any of the zoo's specimens or even

to confirm the Z.I.A.'s existence. Rumors abound that his collection includes centricores, tatzelwurms, crocottas, and other legendary creatures.

Jake skipped the next ten paragraphs in which the author made fun of cryptozoology in general and Dr. Cazador specifically. He had to admit that cryptozoology *did* seem to be a playground for lunatics and scam artists. Finally, Boomswanger brought the article to its brutal conclusion:

> Dr. Cazador, like most frauds, has obviously decided that it is best to shield his "discoveries" from the public where they would be exposed by scientists. Perhaps he's even guilty of animal abuse for exploiting what could be genetically deformed or surgically altered animals.

> A few former employees I spoke to attest to Cazador's brilliance as well as his first-hand familiarity with many of the most remote places in the world. Nevertheless, I believe that the Z.I.A. is far from the harmless pastime of an oddball tycoon. In perpetuating myths about animals that exist only in folktales and freak shows, Dr. Cazador demeans the entire profession of zoology, hurting the cause of science around the world.

Jake was glad that *he* wasn't on William T. Boomswanger's bad side. "Are you *sure* you want to go back the Z.I.A.? I mean, this writer is probably right. Cazador is either a fraud or he's crazy. Either way it's probably not safe to crash his pad."

"Don't tell me you're not curious, Jake," said Miranda. "Let's just try. Afterward, I promise I'll never bring up cryptids or the Z.I.A. again. Besides, you owe me for Handyman."

"All right," he said finally. "We'll give it a shot. Then can we forget Professor Becker, Feng, Bolo, Dr. Cazador, and the Zoo of Impossible Animals?"

"It's a deal!" She wore a bigger smile than he'd seen since they'd left D.C. "Anyway, I realize that it's all nonsense—the cryptids, I mean."

"Sure you do, sis," he said with a grin. "I know you. You're hoping all those weird animals actually exist. You want to play chess with Bigfoot. Surf with the Loch Ness Monster. Ride a unicorn."

Her eyes lit up. "Do you think there might be unicorns?"

"No, I do not," he said. "But I guess there's only one way to find out."

He wished he felt half as confident as he sounded. Unfortunately, he was aware of two things: One, he had *no* idea how they were going to sneak into the Z.I.A., which looked about as well-secured as a military base. Two, he didn't know what they would do when they got caught.

And they *were* going to get caught. Of that, at least, he *did* feel confident.

7

Lunch Date with a Carnivore

T he next morning, Jake knew how they would break into the Z.IA. His idea was bold and original, with just a dash of complete recklessness thrown in to make it exciting.

After their mother left for work, he explained his plan to Miranda. "We can't go through the front gate again," he said as they cleared their plates from breakfast. "I mean, maybe we'd get lucky and Dembi would take us for another ride, but I doubt it. So we sneak in through the back door."

"The back door?" she asked. "What are you talking about?"

"When we first got to Professor Becker's office, Feng mentioned a hole in the fence around the Z.I.A. Do you remember that?"

She snapped her fingers. "Elephant Ridge!"

He nodded. "Exactly. I looked it up before breakfast. Elephant Ridge is on satellite shots I found online. So we just take the trail there, find the hole in the fence, and go in the back way. If we're lucky, we can investigate the zoo before anyone even knows we're there."

"What if Feng already fixed the fence?"

"Then I guess you'll have to go back to your boring calligraphy. What do you say?"

By ten o'clock, they were pedaling down the dirt road to-ward a trail they hoped led to Elephant Ridge. After a few miles, they stopped at the base of a steep hill. A trail curled away from the road up the hill through a bunch of minivan-sized boulders.

"According to the map, this is the trail," he said. "We can ditch our bikes behind one of these rocks. Elephant Ridge should be at the top of the hill."

Two hours later, however, they didn't seem to be any closer to their destination. Jake kept telling Miranda that they were almost there, but with every step he felt more uneasy. The last thing he wanted to do on their first week in New Mexico was to get lost in the desert. He was about to tell her that they should turn back when they saw it—a soaring, barbed-wire fence, identical to the one by Z.I.A.'s front gate. There were several "Keep Out" and "No Trespassing" signs on it, includ-ing one showing a stick-figure person being electrocuted.

"This *must* be it," he said. "Now all we have to do is find that hole in the fence."

"If it still exists," added Miranda.

They walked up and down the fence line, careful to avoid touching it. After a few minutes, Miranda waved him over.

"I think I found it," she said, pointing to a ragged hole that had been created by dirt that had collapsed beneath the fence line. There was barely enough room for them to crawl through, but he could see that it led to the other side. "The hold isn't as big as I expected."

"Are you *sure* you're ready to do this?" he asked.

She shrugged. "It's like you said—we'll be in and out in no time, right? They'll never even know we were here."

"Right," he answered, though he began to feel guilty for helping his sister trespass on private property. After all, he was pretty sure that the worst thing Miranda had ever done was to listen to music on her iPod after their mother told her to go to sleep. "Well, let's check it out."

They ducked carefully through the gap in the fence and hiked through the woods for another fifty yards before emerging from the tree line. The Zoo of Impossible Animals lay below them in the center of a narrow valley. They saw the lake at the north end where two small hills joined together. In the middle of the lake, they saw an island covered in pine trees. Clustered at the south end of the lake sat the enclosures and other buildings, including the tower with the glass house.

"This is going to be a lot harder than we thought," she said. "Look how big it is."

Jake wiped his forehead with his sleeve. It must have been a hundred degrees out. "We've made it this far," he replied. "We might as well see how close we can get."

It took them a half hour to get down to the valley floor. The buildings looked close now, about hundred yards across an area resembling a vast, sunken garden. The garden had several tall trees, large boulders, and lots of low bushes. The wall surrounding it stood only four feet high on the side closest to them, but dropped at least eight feet on the other side.

Jake pointed to a steel ladder built into the wall. "These gardens are the best way in," he said. "If we climb down, nobody will be able to see us. We can walk along the wall until we reach the main buildings."

They climbed down the ladder until they were standing in the garden. Plants, boulders, and trees seemed to have been placed with care and planning. Jake looked up at the high wall above them. What a strange feeling, he thought. Like being at the bottom of an empty swimming pool.

"What a beautiful garden!" exclaimed Miranda. "Let's check it out."

They found a well-worn dirt path that led along the wall and started walking. After a minute or so, they lost sight of the ladder. If they couldn't find a way out on the other side, thought Jake, they would have to turn back.

Suddenly, they stopped. In the middle of the trail, lay a large pile of animal poop. And it looked fresh.

"Gross," he said. "Somebody must have ridden their horse down here."

Miranda frowned. "That's not horse manure. I don't know what kind of animal made that."

They walked on a little farther until they saw a huge bone. It was the kind you would give to a dog, Jake thought. A really big dog.

Suddenly, his whole body froze. "Oh, no!" he said. "How could I have been so stupid?"

"What are you talking about?" asked Miranda, staring at him.

He had been so focused on not being seen by anyone at the zoo that he hadn't realized this wasn't a garden at all. It was an enclosure. An *animal* enclosure.

And they were right in the middle of it.

A feeling of dread crept over him. "I think we're in some kind of animal pen," he said. "A large animal, judging by that poop and the giant bone. We need to get out of here *right now*."

Miranda started to say something when her eyes grew large

with fear. "Behind you," she whispered.

Jake turned around slowly.

In the middle of the path stood a massive tiger, staring at them through blue eyes the color of glacier ice. It was the largest animal he'd ever seen in person— at least ten feet long and maybe 800 pounds. As it moved toward them, the tiger's muscles rippled, its big paws padding the ground silently. It kept its cold, unblinking eyes trained on them, as if it could keep them from moving simply through hypnosis. The animal's mouth and nose were bordered by long whiskers that stuck out on each side like broom bristles. The tiger stopped for a moment. Then it hunched its back and roared, its canines glistening with saliva. The noise was so loud that Jake and Miranda stumbled backwards onto the ground.

"Oh, my gosh," stammered Miranda. "It's... It's..."

"It's blue," he said, finishing her sentence.

The tiger's fur was indeed an outrageous shade of robin's egg blue, interrupted at irregular intervals by black stripes. Its tail twitched behind it as if it had a life of its own.

And before they could even scream, the blue tiger leapt, its front claws bared like eagle talons, its mouth a nightmare of razor-sharp teeth.

3

Saved by a Steak

From somewhere behind them, an object soared through the air above their heads like a flying saucer. But this was no UFO. It was a piece of meat the size of a garbage can lid. In mid-leap, the tiger grabbed the enormous steak in its jaws, landing silently just in in front of them. It sat back on its haunches and tore into the meat, ignoring them completely. They turned to see who had just saved their lives.

On top of the enclosure wall stood the silver-bearded man from the tower. He resembled a mixture between Colonel Sanders and an old-fashioned wizard, thought Jake. He wore a formal white suit with a thin black tie and a wide-brimmed straw hat. He stared down at them, his bushy white eyebrows nearly concealing his dark brown eyes. He leaned on a long, black walking stick. His white hair was so long that it rested on his shoulders.

"Horang-ieke japhyudo jungsinman charimyun sanda," the man said, his voice tinged with a pleasant Spanish accent. "That's a Korean proverb. It means that even if you are caught by a tiger, you can survive by remaining calm." He regarded them with a raised eyebrow. "I don't think it's meant to be applied so literally."

As he spoke, the blue tiger made a contented, yowling

sound, peering up at the man. Then it turned and padded away, the piece of meat still hanging from its jaws. It seemed to melt into the brush, its blue fur blending with the surrounding bushes.

"I found Chung-Mae in the Chang Bai Shan Mountains of North Korea more than a decade ago. Magnificent, isn't she? She is one of the only Maltese blue tigers left in the world. If I hadn't been observing you from my tower, she would have torn both of you apart like tissue paper."

Jake's heart pounded like a jackhammer in his chest. Was this a dream? Did he have heatstroke or something?

The old man tapped his cane on the ground. "Now may I ask what the two of you are doing inside Chung-Mae's enclosure?"

Jake glanced at Miranda, who appeared to be in a state of shock. "It was my fault," he said. "We wanted to see the zoo so we sneaked in. I should have known this was an animal pen. I'm an idiot."

"That much seems indisputable," said the old man dryly. "But it was still a very adventurous attempt. Foolish, but adventurous. And who is your mute companion?"

Miranda, who had been staring up at the man in wonder, managed to shake herself out of her trance. "My name is Miranda," she said. "It's actually my fault for dragging my brother along. *I'm* the one who wanted to see the zoo. I love animals, but I should have known better. I'm sorry."

The old man tilted his head as if seeing them both for the first time. "Might I suggest that you get out of there before Chung-Mae returns? Her appetite is quite insatiable and I don't have any more steaks."

He directed them toward another steel ladder at the far end of the enclosure. Jake let Miranda go up first as he kept his eye out for any signs of the tiger. When it was his turn, he flew up the ladder as if his pants were on fire. When they were both safely out of the enclosure, the old man looked at them, leaning on his long, black staff.

"Professor Becker tells me that two local children found and returned one of our escaped ink monkeys the other day," he said. "May I assume you are they?"

"Actually, Pablo found us," answered Miranda. "He showed up at our house a few days ago. Lost, I guess."

"And hungry," added Jake. "*Really* hungry."

"And so you gave him ink to eat?" asked the old man, skeptically raising one of his silver eyebrows.

"We tried to give him fruit and other stuff," stammered Miranda. "All he wanted was ink." Her face went pale. "He's not dead, is he?"

For the first time, the old man revealed a hint of a smile. "Oh, Pablo is quite well—aside from a terminal case of curiosity. That's a disease both of you appear to suffer from as well." He examined them thoughtfully. "Follow me." He turned and started walking toward the zoo.

Jake and Miranda looked at each other in surprise and then scrambled after him.

"Ink monkeys generally prefer the traditional variety from China, which is made from pine resin and other organic compounds," he explained when they caught up to him. "What exactly did you give him?"

"The first time we saw Pablo, he ate one of Jake's pens," explained Miranda eagerly. "So when we saw him again, I thought he might enjoy my calligraphy ink better, since it's basically a mixture of plant oils and arabic gum."

The man in the suit gave her a sidelong glance, clearly impressed. "Young lady, you caught a cryptid using only your wit and a bottle of ink. Quite extraordinary."

As they walked, Jake stole a glance at their host. Dr. Cazador was several inches taller than he, with deep wrinkles on his face and a dark tan that contrasted with his silver beard and white hair. Despite his age, he looked wiry and strong.

"I don't mean to be nosy," asked Jake, unable to contain himself any longer. "But is your name Dr. Jorge Cazador? Do you own this zoo?"

The old man stopped and pursed his lips, his dark brown eyes studying both of them. "First, you must answer *my* questions. I have only two: Who are you and why are you here?"

Jake rummaged his brain for something clever or funny to say. Instead, he opted for the truth. "My name is Jake Jinks and this is my big sister Miranda," he said, his words tumbling out in a rush. "We just moved to Ranchita from Washington, D.C. We didn't get to see much of the zoo when we brought back Pablo, so we came back to take a look for ourselves."

The old man shook his head. "You have no idea what kinds of animals we have here at the zoo. You could have been killed. In fact, you very nearly were."

"We researched you online first," said Miranda, her voice cracking with emotion. "So we knew you had unusual animals here. I sort of begged Jake to bring me here—he tends to be the braver of the two of us. We just really wanted to meet you. We're sorry. We can walk home if you take us back to the gate."

The old man's eyes softened. "I have some sympathy for

your situation," he said. "I've often gone where I wasn't permitted and found myself in over my head." He tugged at his beard. "My name is Jorge Isidoro de San Luis Cazador and I am, indeed, the owner at the Z.I.A. My keepers usually call me Cazador—or Dr. Cazador if they're feeling very polite. Because you did me the great favor of returning Pablo—who happens to be one of my favorites residents of the Z.I.A.—I will give you a brief tour." Then he paused, holding up a finger to his lips. "However, you must keep what you see here a secret. Is that understood?"

"Loose lips equal one-way trips," said Miranda.

The old man nodded. "Precisely. Anyone who reveals the zoo's secrets is escorted from the premises and never permitted to return. Shall we?"

And with that, they walked quickly down the gravel pathway to the zoo.

9

The Wild World of Cryptids

The Z.I.A. consisted of several long rows of small structures facing one another with gravel pathways connecting them. Jake saw people in tan uniforms doing all sorts of tasks, such as carrying manure in wheel barrows, hauling feed in small trailers, cleaning buildings, and watering plants. Next to the tower stood an enormous aviary covered by thin black netting supported by tall poles. They could see birds flying around inside it.

This is a pretty busy place, thought Jake. Especially if all the effort is for a bunch of made-up animals.

They stopped in front of the first building. "You say you have researched me, *señorita*," said Cazador, peering at Miranda inquisitively. "What did you discover?"

She nodded nervously. "From what I read online, you're the world's most famous cryptozoologist," she replied. "So I assume the Z.I.A. is a zoo for cryptids—creatures not accepted by, um, regular scientists."

"Regular scientists, indeed!" he exclaimed with a snort. "I suppose that is accurate enough. Being a famous cryptozoologist is a bit like being a famous investigator of UFOs or an expert on Atlantis. As far as the outside world is concerned, I'm a con artist or a fool or both. Despite what they say, however, cryptids *are* real."

"Just like UFOs, right?" said Jake sarcastically, shaking his head. "Sorry, doctor. I'm not buying it."

Miranda glared at him. He shrugged. He didn't mean to be rude, but he couldn't have his animal-loving sister tricked into thinking that creatures like blue tigers and ink monkeys actually existed. Tigers can have their fur dyed. Monkeys probably get hungry enough to drink ink. Cheap magic tricks, he thought. There were no more undiscovered animals left in the world.

Cazador caught Jake in a hawk-like stare. To his surprise, though, he didn't seem angry. "I see young Jake is a skeptic. Let's see how long you can maintain your doubts after you meet a few more of my cryptids."

They stopped in front of the next structure. Cazador tapped on the window with his staff. "This is the bakenekos exhibit," he announced. They saw movement inside as animals began to stir. "Bakenekos are the rarest domesticated cats in the world. We found this colony outside a village on the Japanese island of Shikoku."

Jake and Miranda peered into the enclosure. It was the size of their living room, with high ceilings and two large windows on the back wall. Plants, a few small trees, and a dozen wooden posts for climbing were scattered about the room. There appeared to be five or six cats of various colors. Some were brown with white spots or black or red with tan stripes. Their eyes were typical, too—yellow orbs with dark pupils.

"I should warn you," explained Cazador, "Bakenekos are not especially sociable animals, even for cats."

The longer Jake looked, the more it seemed that these were

not cats at all—at least not like any cats he'd ever seen. For one thing, their tails were actually *two* tails. They flicked out behind them like whips, independent of each other. But the second difference was even more bizarre.

"They're walking on their hind legs!" exclaimed Miranda.

It was true. They watched as a brown cat with black spots walked on two legs across one of the horizontal wooden posts carrying a struggling mouse between its front paws. When a yellow cat darted over to it, the brown cat hissed angrily at it. The yellow cat darted out one of its paws in an attempt to steal the mouse, but the brown cat hid the mouse behind its back. After a half a minute, the yellow cat stalked off, its hands folded against its chest in annoyance. Jake and Miranda's mouths hung open as they tried to make sense of what they were seeing.

"Bakenekos are well known in Japanese folklore," continued Cazador. "Their tails split as they grow older, which the Japanese believe turns them into demons." He pointed at the white cat who gazed at them smugly. "That's Ichiro, their leader. He's very full of himself, as you can see."

Near the back of the cage, standing on its hind legs, was a large white cat with black spots on its head. It gazed at them through yellow, unblinking eyes, its two tails swishing behind it. Suddenly, it made a loud yowling sound. The brown cat with the mouse immediately walked over, climbing expertly up the cage. Ichiro held out its paws expectantly and the brown cat reluctantly handed over the mouse. Ichiro began to swing the mouse lazily to and fro like a furry yo-yo. He was showing off!

Jake had seen cats play with their food before, but never like this.

"Did you teach them to walk on two legs like that?" asked Miranda. "It's amazing."

Cazador shook his head. "Have you ever tried to teach a cat *anything*?" he replied. "*Es imposible!* Shall we move along?"

They continued down the path, halting in front of a much larger outdoor enclosure. It was lushly landscaped, with boulders, a small stream, and lots of bamboo trees. The vegetation was so thick that they couldn't see the back wall. A clear, domed roof covered the entire area, which likely explained why it felt so humid standing in front of the viewing window.

"Now where are you?" mumbled Cazador, peering into the enclosure. "My orang mawas are painfully shy, but not usually difficult to spot. They're eight feet tall, after all." He pointed at something. "Ah, there's Eric. Maybe he'll come over and say hello."

A dark tree near the middle of the enclosure shuddered and began to move in their direction. With a start, Jake saw that it wasn't a tree at all but an absurdly tall, ape-like creature. It walked very slowly. Its rail-thin body seemed to consist of a collection of odd angles. Every now and then, the animal had to duck slightly to avoid a tree branch. It had thick black fur and an even thicker mane encircling its head. Yellow teeth jutted from its mouth like the worst overbite of all time.

Jake curled his nose in disgust as a nauseating smell of body odor rose up from the enclosure. Clearly, Eric didn't like to take baths. Under its large brow, the animal's dark, gentle eyes peered out at them for moment. It grunted softly and showed them a long branch as if apologizing for needing to complete some task. Then it turned and strode leisurely toward the other end of the enclosure.

For the first time, Jake considered the possibility that Cazador was telling them the truth. It's one thing to dye a tiger's fur blue or even to split a cat's tail in two and teach it to walk. But how do you stretch an orangutan until it's as tall as a basketball rim?

"We spent ten years searching for the orang mawa," Cazador explained. "The Johor jungle of Malaysia is a very easy place to hide, even for mawas. Unfortunately, some angry villagers found them first. We had to purchase Eric and Priya from the village chieftain for a million ringitts."

Miranda stared at the departing creature in awe. "I've never heard of an orang mawa. It's so tall! It reminds me of, well, one of those, you know…"

"A wookie," said Jake. "Like Chewbacca from Star Wars."

"No, not a wookie," she said, frowning at him. "A yeti. A sasquatch. You know—Big Foot."

Cazador nodded approvingly. "Very observant, Miranda. In my expert opinion, those hominid cryptids are indeed close relatives of the mawa. As are the Nguoi Rung rock apes of Vietnam and Laos."

When the doctor saw Jake's flabbergasted expression, he sighed. "What? You don't believe undiscovered mountain apes exist? That's all Sasquatch is. Most specimens at the Z.I.A. are either undiscovered, unbelievable, or thought to be extinct. Those characteristics are what make them cryptids and not hippos or pandas or any number of God's more boring creatures."

They stopped next at another outside pen. It actually seemed to be two pens, divided in half by an almost invisible wire fence. The entire area was roughly the size of the blue tiger enclosure. Six or seven sand-colored deer rested in the shade of a boulder on the left side of the enclosure. They weren't large—about the size of sheep—but their heads were strong and almost oblong-shaped. One stretched its neck up to nibble the green leaves from the lower branches of a tree.

"Oh," said Jake, unable to hide his disappointment. "They're just gazelles."

"No, I think they're Arabian oryx," said Miranda, staying positive as always. "Or maybe sable antelopes? I've seen them at the National Zoo. They're very rare."

"They *are* rare," said Cazador. "However, I don't think you've ever seen these particular animals at any zoo. Look more closely."

Miranda and Jake leaned against the metal bar separating the higher viewing area from the enclosure. The animals were milling about the enclosure and one of them moved closer to the viewing stand. It looked up at them and made a weird, high pitched noise like a baby crying. Then it rubbed its slender horns against one of the trees. The horns glinted in the sunlight like skinny rods of gold.

Exactly like rods of gold, thought Jake. "Am I seeing things or do those things they have golden horns?" he asked, realizing how silly he sounded.

"Fourteen karat!" exclaimed Cazador proudly. "These are goldhorn antelopes, the legendary chamois bucks of eastern Europe. Many centuries ago there were herds of them in Slovenia and Carinthia. Sadly, their most beautiful quality led to their demise." He shook his head. "Such has been the case with so many species, from the white rhino to the wooly mammoth to the unicorn."

Miranda's eyes lit up. "Are there really unicorns? Are you serious? Do you have one here?"

Cazador seemed not to hear her. Instead, he pointed to the horse-like animals in the other half of the enclosure. "Do you see the two larger animals on the other side of the electric fence? Tell me what you see."

There were two animals with long horns and dark brown fur coats playing together. They were nearly as large as moose. Each one had a pair of long horns that looked sharp enough to punch a hole in a car door. As they dueled, their horns seemed to move on their head. Jake blinked to make sure he wasn't hallucinating. He looked again. Sure enough, one of their horns swiveled and turned while the other would align itself and join the fight or point backwards.

Miranda pointed at the deer excitedly. "Their horns move in different directions!" she exclaimed. "How is that possible?"

"These are two of only a handful of centricores left in the entire world," said Cazador. "One is a buck and the other is a ewe. Unfortunately, they don't like each other very much, so we have no centricore fawns yet. We found them in the Vercors foothills of the Alps after we got reports of horned monsters attacking the local cattle."

"They went after cows?" asked Miranda, appalled. "Why would they do *that?*"

Cazador shrugged. "I suppose because they're carnivorous," he said. "Centricores are quite dangerous when they're hungry or threatened. It has to do with the second law of cryptozoology: 'Cryptids vigorously defend their territory.' It's why we have to keep an electric fence between them and the goldhorns. If the centricores get hungry enough, they'd eat them up. They'd probably leave the gold, though."

They walked to the next enclosure. This one belonged to a black, green-eyed jaguar who sprawled upon the branch of a large tree. The creature was nearly as long as Chung-Mae, thought Jake, but not nearly as scary looking. Maybe because he wasn't trying to eat them. One of the jaguar's oversized paws hung off the branch as it gazed at them lazily through half-lidded eyes. It yawned, revealing long white teeth and a pink tongue. Its fur was completely black except for a white spot in the shape of crescent moon on its shoulder.

"This is Javier," said Cazador, gesturing with his staff. "As you might expect, he's not an ordinary black jaguar. He's a cryptid called a *balam,* now found only in the most remote rainforests of Honduras. The balam is one of the chief gods of Maya people, or at least he was 500 years ago. That white spot on his shoulder waxes and wanes with the moon. It's only a sliver right now because the moon is a waning crescent. When the moon is full, you can see that spot from a hundred yards away. Quite remarkable."

As Cazador spoke, Jake spied a black golf cart speeding down the hill toward them from the administration buildings. His heart sank. It was Alan Feng. He tapped Miranda on the shoulder. "Look who's here. It's Mr. Sunshine."

"Oh, no!" she groaned. "He's going to ruin everything."

Feng's cart skidded noisily to a stop in front of them, kicking up a small cloud of dust. The squat, sour-faced Feng scowled at them as he got out of his cart and walked over to Cazador. The doctor was still remarking on Javier's birthmark.

"Ahem," said Feng, clearing his throat loudly. "Dr. Cazador, may I speak with you for a moment?"

Cazador stopped in mid-sentence and looked at him. "Oh, hello, Alan. I didn't see you arrive. What can I do for you?"

"I came as soon as I learned of the security breach," he said, frowning at Miranda and Jake. "It's my recommendation, doctor, that we prosecute these two delinquents to the fullest extent of the law. It's the only way they'll ever learn. I've already informed the Ranchita Police, who should be—"

Cazador held up his hand. "Did you know that these two children waltzed past our electrified fencing as if it weren't even there?" he said. "What is the point of all this expensive, new security equipment if it doesn't even work? Things are getting sloppy around here, Alan. It's no wonder cryptids keep disappearing."

Feng nodded. "I asked Bolo to investigate the fence issue, doctor. He refused, so I told Dembi to take care of it. But getting back to the trespassers—"

"I hardly think it is Dembi's job to repair fences," said Cazador, interrupting him again. "He's not a handyman, he's a cryptid hunter. One of our finest, I might add."

"Of course, sir," began Feng, who was getting increasingly frustrated. "But regarding these trespassing children—"

"In fact, the next time a cryptid goes missing, I will come to you *personally* for answers," said Cazador. "We cannot afford another incident like last year when our ngoima devoured those poor sheep at that woman's farm in Ranchita."

"Believe me, sir, the security of the Z.I.A. is of paramount importance to me," he sputtered. "As I mentioned, though, the police are at the front gate waiting for us—"

"Ah, yes, the police," said Cazador brusquely. "Apologize to them for wasting their time and tell them you will *not* be contacting them with such frivolous requests in the future. You know I never involve the authorities in zoo business."

"Frivolous requests?" said Feng incredulously, his face now as red as a tomato. "Dr. Cazador, I hardly think that such wanton disregard—"

"Oh, and one final item, Mr. Feng," interrupted Cazador for the fifth time. "Go find two uniforms for the Jinks children. They will be our new tyros this summer. The girl is obviously a genius and the boy has the makings of a top-notch cryptid hunter. They start Monday."

Jake didn't know who seemed more surprised by this news—Feng or them. They stared at Cazador, jaws agape.

Cazador glanced down at his watch. "Where has the time gone?" he exclaimed. "I must tend to a desperately ill blob fish in our aquarium." He turned to Jake and Miranda. "Dembi will drive you home. I'll look for you here on Monday morning at 8 o'clock. Do not be late."

With that, he turned and walked briskly toward a large building down by the lake. Feng shot them a final nasty look and hurried after him.

Jake and Miranda stared at each other, too stunned to speak. Within a short span of time, they had gone from being trespassers, to being the youngest cryptozoologists at the world's most amazing zoo. Now they just needed to convince their mother to let them take the job.

And how hard could that be? thought Jake.

10

Mothers and Other Fierce Creatures

By the time they got home, Miranda had still not stopped gushing about their job offer, even though neither of them knew exactly what a tyro was. Jake, on the other hand, had come back down to Earth, emotionally speaking. He now felt certain their mother would *never* let them work at the Z.I.A. It just didn't look good on paper: weird private zoo, reclusive billionaire, potentially deadly animals, giant electric fence. Their mother wasn't going to like any of it. Miranda, on the other hand, felt that if they pushed the "learning experience" angle as hard as they could, she'd have to let them do it.

When their mother got home that evening, they had salad and spaghetti waiting for her. Miranda even found some wild roses growing in the front yard and stuffed them in a vase, which she placed in the middle of the table. Jake had never seen his sister more determined to succeed at something.

"What a wonderful surprise!" said their mother as she sat down. "I don't remember the last time you two made dinner. In fact, I don't think you've ever made dinner. Are things so boring around here that you've taken up cooking?"

"Not at all, Mom," said Miranda. "I mean, sure, there's no cable and we don't have cell phones, or summer camps, or friends, but we're still having fun. Right, Jake?"

"Right," he replied, following the script they'd worked out earlier. Just stay positive, his sister had told him. "We're relaxing and reevaluating our brains out."

"We've actually been riding our bikes a lot," continued Miranda. "And hiking. You know—checking out the area, seeing the sights. Exploring all the amazing things the area has to offer."

"How nice," said their mother, clearly surprised. "Where have you gone? Not too far off the property, I hope. Do we have any neighbors?"

"Funny you should ask," said Jake slowly. "A few days ago we learned that there's a private zoo right here in Ranchita. We went to check it out and—this is the fantastic part—the owner offered us summer jobs starting on Monday. How great is that, right? What an incredible learning opportunity!"

Their mother stopped eating and put down her fork. "You went to a private zoo?" she said, her voice rising. "Without asking me? Maybe both of you should start from the beginning."

They told her everything. Well, almost everything, thought Jake. They had agreed beforehand not to offer up too many details about the cryptids. Mostly because Cazador had sworn them to secrecy, but also because they knew their mother would freak out.

"We're even getting uniforms with our names on them and everything," concluded Miranda eagerly. "It's the educational chance of a lifetime!"

Jake thought they were overdoing it a little, but he sensed that their mother was seriously considering it. His heart soared with hope.

Then Miranda completely forgot about the "no details" rule.

"Dr. Cazador is an amazing man, Mom," she said. "He saved us from this amazing blue tiger after we accidentally climbed into its pen. He tossed a big steak to it and it just walked away. My heart was beating so fast! It's the most beautiful animal I've ever seen."

Jake shot her a "please-shut-up-now" look, but the damage had been done.

Their mother's face darkened ominously. "Wait a second," she began slowly. "Are you telling me that you literally climbed into a pen with a tiger in it—"

"A blue tiger," said Miranda, who suddenly knew she'd said too much.

"—a blue tiger in it, and this Dr. Cazador had to toss a piece of raw meat to it so that you wouldn't be eaten alive?"

Jake tried a forced laugh. "You make it sound more dramatic than it was, Mom," he said. "It wasn't a big deal. I mean, sure, *I* might have been a goner, but Miranda would have made it out alive. I mean, how much kid can one tiger eat, right?"

Their mother didn't even crack a smile.

That's not a good sign, he thought.

Miranda now had a panicked look on her face. "Anyway, everything worked out fine," she said. "No big deal. Did you know it's probably the last blue tiger in the entire world? You should have seen it, Mom."

But their mother wasn't listening any more. Her face took

on an unhealthy shade of violet. Her jaw clenched and un-clenched as if she were gnawing on barbed wire. Jake thought he might have actually heard her growl.

"I don't care if the tiger was blue, yellow, or neon pink," she said, a menacing edge to her voice. "You both could have been killed. And you—" She glared at Miranda. "You're almost fifteen years old! What in the world were you thinking, involving your brother in this? You're supposed to be the responsible one. You not supposed to encourage his reckless behavior!"

"Hello? I'm sitting right here!" said Jake, still trying to inject some humor into the tense situation. "Besides, one person's reckless is another person's awesome."

Miranda was practically in tears now. "Jake and I can take care of ourselves, Mom," she said. "Isn't that what we've always done, with you working all the time? We just wanted to see the animals. Dr. Cazador would be a great boss to have for a summer. It would give us something to do."

Their mother pressed her hand against her forehead as if in pain. "It doesn't matter now. The important thing is that you're both OK. But there is no way I'm going to allow you anywhere near such dangerous animals. The Z.I.A. is obviously no place for kids."

"That's not fair!" protested Miranda, her voice rising. "There nothing around here except for the Z.I.A. We could study zoology and conservation and—"

"I'm done discussing this with you, young lady," their mother said sternly. "I'm very disappointed in both of you. You might think you're adults these days, but you're still just kids. This kind of behavior makes that crystal clear."

Miranda burst into tears and leaped up from the table. She

ran up the stairs to her room. Jake took a bite of his spaghetti, which now tasted flavorless and nauseating. Like my life, he thought.

His mother and he ate the rest of the meal in silence, except for the sounds of Miranda sobbing in her room above them.

11

Farewell to the Z.I.A.

The rest of the weekend was extremely uncomfortable for everyone. Miranda spent most of her time in her room. Jake could hear her occasionally talking to herself. When their mother tried to speak to her, she acted sulky and withdrawn. The summer of relaxing and reevaluating had suddenly become the summer of moping and mourning.

For his part, Jake knew better than to argue with his mom about her decision. He'd learned that once she'd made up her mind there was no changing it. Actually, he thought, she and Miranda were similar in that way, which explained the current unpleasantness. He spent most of his time playing video games and trying not to think about ink monkeys, Cazador, or the Z.I.A.

By the time Monday morning finally rolled around, their mother looked relieved to be going back to work. "I'll be slammed at the clinic today," she said, grabbing her white doctor's jacket. "I probably won't get back until after seven. I'll pick up dinner in Ranchita on the way home. Does pizza sound good?"

"Sure," said Jake. "Sounds great."

Miranda glumly stirred her bowl of cereal at the table. "Whatever," she said. "It doesn't matter."

Their mother sighed. "Look, honey, you'll get over this. I'll find something else for you to do."

"Like what?" asked Miranda, looking up at her. "What else is there in Ranchita besides an unbelievably amazing zoo? I guess I could go work down at the fertilizer store. I'm sure that will be just as fun."

Their mother frowned. "You'll think of something. Isn't that right, Jake?"

Wrong, he thought. "Right," he said. "We'll be fine. See you tonight."

"That's the attitude," she said. "Call me if you need anything."

When she was gone, he glanced over at Miranda, who looked as if she might cry again. "I have an idea that might cheer you up. Let's ride over to the Z.I.A. one last time. I mean, Cazador is expecting us to show up this morning, right? The least we can do is to go there in person to let him know that we can't work there this summer."

She looked up from her cereal hopefully. "Really? But what if Mom finds out?"

He shrugged. "We're not going there to hang out with the animals, right? Besides, if we leave right now we'll be back way before she gets home."

"You're right," she said eagerly. "We'll just go there and tell Dr. Cazador that our mom won't let us work at his zoo and then we'll come back home. We're just being polite. It's almost something she'd want us to do."

"Exactly!" he agreed. "Otherwise, he might think we're ungrateful jerks."

She nodded. "But let's leave Mom a note and directions to

the zoo, just in case. If she comes back early, she might freak out if we aren't here. We'll have plenty of time to get rid of the note when we get back."

"Good idea," he said. "So what are we waiting for? I'll get the bikes."

When they arrived at the Z.I.A.'s front gate, a zoo guard awaited them in one of the black golf carts. They left their bikes by the gate and he drove them to the zoo, dropping them off in front of the tower with the glass building on top.

"Just take the elevator to the third floor," he told them. "That's Cazador's office. It's his house, too, actually. Mr. Feng is already up there."

"OK, thanks," said Miranda. "But we really just stopped by to tell—"

"Oh, sorry," he interrupted, glancing at his cell phone. "Mohan's shift is over. I've got to get back to the guard room. Good luck this summer, tyros! I'll see you around." He sped up the road back toward the administration buildings.

Jake and Miranda stepped off the elevator into a command center of some kind. The room looked completely open, encircled by floor-to-ceiling windows that overlooked the valley. There were a half-dozen people working at desks with giant computer consoles on them. Several were speaking on phones in various languages. There were two oversized leather couches near a kitchen area. A set of spiral stairs near the elevator led up to what must have been another floor.

"There's Feng," said Miranda. "Over there by those three huge computer screens. I suppose we should go over and talk to him."

"I guess so," Jake mumbled. "He's the only person who will

be happy we won't be working here this summer."

But before they could approach him, Feng looked up and saw them. He made a sour face. He barked a command to someone at one of the desks, who brought over a package and handed it to him. Feng strode over to them. He held two tan uniforms in his arms.

He shoved the clothes into Jake's chest. "You're late for your first day," he said. "Don't let it happen again. Use the locker rooms in the aquarium. Both of you are to report to Professor Becker by the fountain in the main plaza."

"Actually, Mr. Feng," began Miranda. "We just came to let Dr. Cazador know that we won't be able to work at the Z.I.A. this summer after all. Our Mom thinks it's too dangerous."

"Even though it's obviously not," Jake added defiantly.

Feng's mood brightened immediately. "Is that so?" he said. "That's the best news I've heard all week! I'll take those back, thank you." He snatched the uniforms out of Jake's hands.

"Somehow we knew you wouldn't be too upset," said Miranda sullenly. "We'll just thank Dr. Cazador and leave."

"There's no need for that," Feng replied coldly. He took out his cell phone and pressed a button. "I'll pass along your regrets to him myself. I'll have a guard take you back to the gate. Arnel? We need a cart to the tower immediately. I need you to take—"

He was interrupted by the sounds of yelling near the elevator. It was a woman's voice, thought Jake, and she sounded angry. Suddenly, the elevator doors slid open and two security guards burst out of it. They were closely followed by a woman who looked a lot like—

"Mom!" they exclaimed.

12

Mom Crashes the Zoo

Don't tell me I can't be here!" their mother yelled at the guards. She jabbed a finger at the tall one's chest. "You couldn't keep me away from my children, even if this tower were a thousand feet high!"

"That's fine, ma'am," stammered the guard. "We just need to understand how you got in. We never got a call from the front gate."

"I called three times!" she shouted. "Some idiot told me that there were no kids allowed at the zoo, even though I could see the bikes leaning against the fence. So I climbed your gate. *Now where are my children?*"

This should be interesting, thought Jake. "Hi, Mom," he said. "I guess you got our note. Why are you back from work so early?"

"I left my cell phone at home," she said, striding over to where they were standing. "You need to tell me *right now* why you came over here when I expressly told you not to."

"We weren't going to stay long," said Miranda quickly. "We just wanted to let Dr. Cazador know that we wouldn't be working here this summer."

"Even though they gave us uniforms with our names on them," said Jake.

"But I took them back, didn't I?" interjected Feng with a smug grin. "By the way, Mrs. Jinks, I think you've made an excellent decision. You saved the Z.I.A. from making a huge mistake."

"It *wouldn't* have been a mistake," said Miranda angrily. "We would have done a great job."

Their mother frowned. "I'm sure they would have made fine interns, Mr. Feng," she said. "The reason I don't want them working here is because of all the dangerous animals." She paused. "And it's *Dr.* Jinks, by the way. And you are?"

"Alan Feng, assistant director," he said smoothly. "You're absolutely correct, Dr. Jinks. It's far too dangerous for children—especially *your* children. Now if you'll excuse me, I have work to do."

Behind them, the elevator opened again and Cazador stepped out of it, followed by Professor Becker. "Dr. Jinks!" exclaimed the doctor, as if greeting an old friend. "I'm so glad finally to meet you in person. I've heard so much about you."

"Um, hello," she said, confused. "I don't think we've met. Are you the owner of the zoo?"

"I am indeed," he said, bowing slightly. "My name is Dr. Jorge Isidoro de San Luis Cazador, but please call me Cazador. This is the zoo's director, Professor Markus Becker. Why don't you sit down for a moment?"

They followed Cazador and Becker into the kitchen. To their surprise, Pablo crouched on Cazador's shoulder. When the ink monkey saw Miranda, he squeaked and ran down the doctor's arm and over to her. She picked him up and cradled him in her arms, giving him a gentle squeeze.

"Good morning, Pablo," she said. "I missed you."

Cazador sat down at a table and removed his straw hat. He leaned his black staff against a wall. "Did Jake and Miranda discuss the offer I made to them on Friday?"

"They did," she replied, sitting down in one of the chairs. "They told me that you hired them to work at your zoo this summer. That is very generous of you."

He nodded curtly. "Judging by the fact that you are here and obviously quite perturbed, may I assume that you told them 'no' and they decided to come anyway?"

"That's right," she said, eyeing Miranda and Jake with obvious annoyance. "I'm afraid I can't have them working here this summer. I'm starting a new job at a very busy clinic in Sandoval. I don't feel comfortable having them work in such an unsafe environment. I hope you understand."

He smiled and glanced at Professor Becker, exchanging a quick look with him. "It's quite a relief to hear you say that, Dr. Jinks," he said. "Actually, the professor and I intended to withdraw our offer this morning and I did not relish breaking the bad news to your children. Thank you for saving us the need to do so."

Jake felt like he had been punched in the stomach. He glanced over at Miranda, who look stunned.

"Oh, I see," said their mother, slightly confused. "That's good, I guess. Out of curiosity, what made you change your mind?"

"We decided that being a tyro at an elite scientific research institution such as the Z.I.A. is simply too challenging for children," explained Cazador. "My intention had been for Jake and Miranda to handle only the most harmless of the zoo's specimens, working closely with the senior keepers. However,

I now feel that even this limited role is beyond them."

Beyond us? thought Jake indignantly. He sounded exactly like Feng!

"Well, actually, doctor, Miranda has studied a lot of science for a ninth grader," said their mother. "She even volunteered at the National Zoo last winter. And Jake is my adventurous child—always eager to learn. Mind you, I'm still opposed to the idea of them working here, but I think they would have made excellent, um, tyros at your zoo. Is that like an intern?"

"You may be correct about your daughter," replied Cazador, ignoring her question. "She has already demonstrated by her capture of Pablo that she's extremely intelligent and resourceful. However, your son is another story, no?" He gave Jake a look that made him want to crawl under the table.

Professor Becker removed a manila folder from his bag. "We took the liberty of contacting the school that Jake most recently atttended," he said. "His former principal—Mrs. Mora, is it?—felt that he was 'undisciplined and rebellious, though quite intelligent, with untapped leadership skills.' She also found his propensity for playing practical jokes highly disruptive. In her opinion—"

"Actually, Professor Becker," interrupted their mother. "Jake acts up only when he's bored, which has been most of the time over the past few years. Part of that has been my fault for not paying as much attention to him as I should. However, when he has the proper motivation, he always rises to the challenge." She paused. "And Principal Mora has no sense of humor at all."

What's going on here? thought Jake. For someone who had told them a few days ago that she would never let them work at the zoo, their mom seemed to be trying her hardest to get their job back.

Cazador scratched his beard thoughtfully. "You make some interesting points, Dr. Jinks," he said. "I agree that the educational experience *would* benefit your children, which is why I made my offer. And I suppose Alan *did* already have uniforms made them—"

"I can easily remove their names, Dr. Cazador," interrupted Feng. He looked dismayed at the sudden change in the tenor of the conversation. "Really, sir, it would be no problem for me to—"

"If you permit them to work at your zoo this summer," said their mother, cutting off Feng, "I promise that they will make all the necessary sacrifices and act professionally." She turned to Miranda and Jake. "Do I have your word on that?"

They stared at her in stunned disbelief for a moment. "Yes!" they shouted at the same time.

Cazador threw up his hands and smiled. "Who am I to argue with such eloquence?" he exclaimed. "I surrender! Jake and Miranda shall begin their tyroships tomorrow, provided they work diligently, listen to their supervising keepers, and scrupulously avoid the few dangerous animals we have on the premises. I'm so glad you stopped by, Dr. Jinks. I will have someone escort the three of you back to the gate."

As Cazador and Becker walked back to the elevator, Jake and Miranda gave their mother a hug. Feng threw the uniforms onto the table in disgust and stormed off. As Jake watched Cazador waiting for the elevator, the old man saw him staring and winked, giving him the thumbs-up sign.

With a start, Jake suddenly realized that Cazador *never* intended to revoke the offer at all. The whole scene had been staged to convince their mother to change her mind. It was the most brilliant acting he'd seen in his life!

And thanks to the doctor's performance, he and Miranda were the newest—and youngest—tyros at the Zoo of Impossible Animals.

13

Support Your Local Sea Serpent

After breakfast the next day, Jake and Miranda got on their bikes and headed to the zoo. When they arrived at the front gate, Dembi was waiting for them. He signaled for them to join him in the black golf cart. They left their bikes and drove with him to the aquarium.

"There's the blue tiger enclosure!" exclaimed Miranda after Dembi dropped them off. "Let's go say hello to Chung-Mae."

"Mom said that *you're* supposed to be the responsible one, remember?" replied Jake. "Actually, I *do* want to check out that blue beast again. I think I'll enjoy him a lot more if I'm *outside* the enclosure. But Dembi told us to hang out at the aquarium."

Actually, Dembi hadn't told them anything because that would mean he had actually *spoken,* which he hadn't. He just pointed to the name on the building that read "Aquarium," made a sign with his hand indicating a long beard, pointed at them, and then at the ground. The message was clear enough: "Wait here for Dr. Cazador."

It felt as hot as an oven outside as they waited in the shade of the building. They looked out at the lake. It stretched from one side of the valley to the other and another half mile toward the hills that marked the valley's end.

"I'm going to burst into flames out here," Jake said, wiping the sweat already forming on his forehead. "Maybe we should go inside. Dr. Cazador might already be in there."

Inside, the aquarium seemed as large as a warehouse, with tall windows overlooking the lake. Surprisingly, the building didn't have a back wall. Instead, it opened directly onto the lake and even seemed connected to it. They could smell water, fish, and wet soil in the air.

In the center of the giant room stood the most massive fish tank they had ever seen. The glass structure looked to be twenty feet high and as long and wide as a basketball court. It seemed big enough to park a dozen dump trucks. It had a sandy bottom with coral and rock formations around which countless fish swam.

Miranda pointed to a person in a tan Z.I.A. uniform. "Let's ask that guy if he knows where Cazador is," she said.

As they got closer, they saw that the man was tossing softball-sized frogs into a swamp-like enclosure filled with ferns, cypress trees, vines, and two or three moss-encrusted boulders. The keeper finally noticed them and put down his bucket. He wiped his hands on his pants and shook their hands. He was a very short Asian man, with close-cropped black hair and a friendly face.

"Good morning, tyros!" he said, smiling broadly. "My name is Tuan Ngyuen. You are looking for Cazador, yes?"

"Yes," Jake replied as Miranda warily eyed a long centipede crawling around inside a container at the man's feet. "He told us to meet him at the aquarium. Have you seen him this morning?"

"He's out there," said Tuan, gesturing toward the lake. "He told me all about you. You were the kids who caught Pablo. Such a naughty monkey. You will learn many things here!"

"What are you doing with those frogs, Mr. Ngyuen?" asked Miranda. "They don't seem like cryptids to me. What's so special about them?"

"Maybe they glow in the dark," offered Jake, grinning.

Tuan shook his head. "Frogs aren't cryptids. Frogs are food for salamanders. See down there?"

He pointed to the edge of the pool where the vegetation grew most thickly. Jake and Miranda looked in wonder as four peach-colored animals scuttled out of the undergrowth. At first, Jake thought they were alligators—they were just as long and crawled along on their bellies. Their skin looked moist and leathery and they had pea-sized, orange eyes with mouths wide enough to swallow a dog. Their heads were wide and flat, almost as if a steamroller had flattened them. They dragged themselves into the water using stubby arms and legs and delicate, four-fingered paws that were almost human-like. Their fleshy tails propelled them through the water as they made a beeline toward the frogs.

"They're pink!" exclaimed Miranda approvingly. "I've never seen pink salamanders."

"I've never seen salamanders as big as alligators, either," said Jake. "They're pretty gross. What are they again?"

"Giant pink salamanders from Japan," Tuan announced proudly. "Dr. Cazador is trying to breed them with the black ones. No luck so far."

Jake was about to ask which black ones he was talking about when a log moved to their left. With a start, they realized that the log was actually a creature as big as a Komodo dragon. It seemed a lot like the pink salamanders that were still making their way across the pond, but it had skin the color of coal and creepy, evil-looking yellow eyes. It looked twice as large as the pink ones. It half-rolled, half-waddled its way toward the frogs, which were now frantically hopping in the other direction. With surprising quickness, the black salamander lunged, grabbing one of the frogs in its jaws. In a single gulp, it disappeared down the salamander's gullet.

"I hope you're enjoying the show," said a friendly voice behind them.

They turned. In front of them, hands clasped behind his back, stood the towering figure of Professor Markus Becker. He wore his perfectly pressed khaki zoo uniform, his thin blond hair slicked back neatly against his head. Alan Feng and the man with the scar and tattoos named Bolo were standing behind him.

"I've told Dr. Cazador that the Trinity Alps specimens will never take to the Japanese Pinks," he said cheerily. "But he's forever adopting such misfits, either out of pity or sheer stubbornness. I suppose that's why he's the genius and we're all just trying to keep up." He glanced at Tuan, who seemed to be flustered to see the zoo director there. "If you're finished here, Tuan, why don't you assist Karlie with the squonks. Alan tells me they're particularly emotional today. Why don't you give them an extra helping of the white truffles?"

"Good idea, Professor," Tuan replied. "I'll do that right now." He hastily gathered up the empty containers, and walked toward the aquarium exit.

When he left, Professor Becker smiled at them. "I'm so

glad Cazador asked you to join us at the Z.I.A. this summer," he said. "I admit I had my doubts at first, but I think it will be quite a rewarding experience for both of you. Don't you agree, Alan?"

"Not really," said Feng grumpily. "But no one around here seems to care what I think."

The professor frowned at his assistant director. "You'll have to forgive Mr. Feng," he told Jake and Miranda. "He'll warm up to you eventually. In the meantime, if either of you needs anything while you're here, please don't hesitate to ask me. I'll do whatever I can to help. And congratulations again on being the youngest tyros in the history of the Z.I.A. You should be quite proud of yourselves." He smiled again and then turned and walked out of the aquarium.

Bolo and Feng lingered, staring at Jake and Miranda. "Dr. Cazador and the professor may not mind having you here," said Feng. "But *I* do. Don't screw up or I'll have you shipped out of here so fast you won't have time to wipe the manure off your shoes."

Miranda frowned. "We'll keep that in mind," she said.

"And thanks for the image," said Jake. "I'm going to be a lot more careful of where I walk around here now."

Bolo traced his finger idly along the scar on his cheek. "You could introduce 'em to a Mongolian death worm, Alan," he said. "I bet they'd be *real* interested in one those."

Feng scowled at the large man. "You talk too much, Bolo. Let's go."

"I'm just trying to make our new tyros feel at home," said Bolo, grinning. "You need to lighten up, Feng."

"Why does everyone keep telling me that?" said Feng. He

turned and walked toward the exit.

"See you around, kids," said Bolo, winking at them. He turned and followed the assistant director out the door.

"What a couple of weirdoes," said Jake when the two men were gone. "Professor Becker seems OK, though."

"Yes, he's really nice," she said. "Hey, look! That must be Cazador."

They walked quickly over to the far end of the aquarium behind the fish tank where a dock extended into the lake. Several people in wet suits were climbing up a ladder onto the dock. Despite his wet suit, oxygen tank, and snorkel mask, they could see it was Cazador because of his long silver beard and hair.

"Welcome!" said the doctor. "I'm so pleased you're here at last. I was concerned that your mother might be reluctant to let you come. I'm glad she visited us in person so I could help you make your case. What a lovely woman!"

"I don't know how you did it, doctor," said Miranda. "But somehow you changed her mind. That was pretty cool."

"You definitely bailed us out," agreed Jake. "I was going to have to spend the entire summer reading my aunt's old gardening catalogues."

Cazador waved his hand. *"De nada,"* he said. "Think nothing of it. I'm just happy she relented. And I *will* need your assistance this summer. My zoo has fallen into disarray lately. I've not been as attentive as I should. Too many overseas trips searching for cryptids, I'm afraid."

A stocky, bearded man climbed out of the lake and onto the dock. He held a long pole with a sharp silver tip at the end of it.

"You were spearfishing?" asked Miranda. "Did you catch

anything?"

"We weren't really fishing," replied the doctor. "We're searching for Lola. We haven't seen her in two months and we've grown quite worried. The spear gun is just for our protection. You know, in case the giant eels get too—what's the word?—*frisky.*"

"Who's Lola?" asked Miranda.

Cazador removed his oxygen tank and then his fins. "Lola is the Z.I.A.'s resident sea serpent," he replied. "With the possible exception of Pablo, she's my favorite animal at the zoo. In fact, we named the lake after her."

"Right," said Jake, grinning. He assumed this was a joke they played on all new employees. "So what's wrong with her? Does she have the flu?"

"Perhaps. We're not sure," said Cazador, gazing out at the lake pensively. "Cormick believes she's pregnant, which *would* explain why she's staying in deep water. But since she's the only one of her kind in the lake, I'm not sure how she could manage *that* trick. I suppose she could be parthenogenetic. She *is* a lizard, after all."

"Oh, she's preggers all right," interrupted the bulky, dark-haired man who had emerged from the lake after Cazador. He had a thick Scottish accent and a short beard. With his black wetsuit, he resembled a cross between a lumberjack and a sea lion. "That's why she's stayin' outta sight. The ruddy eels are making nuisances o' themselves again and she wants to have her wee bairn in peace. Can't blame her for that, can we?"

He grinned at them, revealing large white teeth that seemed capable of biting through wire. He clapped Jake on the shoulder. "Don't worry, laddie. The arapaima keep the eels from gettin' outta hand." He looked at Cazador. "We ne'er should have brought those eels down from Newfoundland, doctor. Disgusting creatures, they are. They don't even taste good."

"I'm sure they feel the same way about you, Cormick," said Cazador good-naturedly. "But where are my manners? Jake and Miranda, this is Cormick Mackenzie. Jake, you'll be working with him on the lake and here in the aquarium. He's from Scotland, as he will remind you constantly. It will take you most of the summer just to understand him."

Cormick shook Jake and Miranda's hands. "Och! It'll be my pleasure to school ye. Breaking in tyros is my favorite pastime. I'll have ye speaking proper English by the end o' summer! See you in a twink." He grabbed his oxygen tank and fins and walked toward a set of doors in one of the far walls.

"We've been meaning to ask you, doctor," began Miranda. "What *is* a tyro exactly?"

"It's a new recruit—an intern," said Cazador. "Our tyros are usually foolish, frightened, and more trouble than they're worth. I'm sure the two of you will be exceptions. The fact that you managed to capture Pablo and then find your way back into my top-secret zoo makes me think you have the makings of top-notch cryptozoologists."

"Getting back to your sea serpent," asked Jake, who wanted to see how far Cazador would take a joke. "How did she end up in your lake? I mean, you didn't find her here, right?"

"Heavens, no!" he exclaimed. "Her species doesn't exist in North America, as far as we know. She's from a lake in Neuquén, Patagonia, not far from my hometown. We think she must be some kind of relative of a plesiosaur. I saw her mother and father once when I was a child. Let me tell you—it was no small feat bringing Lola to New Mexico. Imagine transporting a gray whale with a neck as long as a telephone pole and you get the idea."

"A plesiosaur?" said Miranda incredulously. "But they're extinct!"

Cazador shook his head. "It turns out they're only *mostly* extinct," he said.

Jake frowned. "That makes no sense. How can an animal be *mostly* extinct?"

The old man slipped on his sandals. "Let me show you something. Come with me."

They walked over to the enormous fish tank. Cazador pointed to an awkward-looking, glassy-eyed fish swimming slowly along the sandy bottom.

"That is a coelacanth," he said. "Scientists told us that this species became extinct 65 million years ago. And that's what everyone believed—until a fisherman caught one off the coast of South Africa in 1938. You see? The coelacanth was only *mostly* extinct."

The fish was about seven feet long, with white blotches all over its otherwise black scales. It had lots of fins—two on top, two below, four on each side. It glided slowly through the water with the help of a single, oversized back fin. Its mouth hung open slightly revealing two rows of tiny teeth.

That is one ugly fish, thought Jake.

"So the coelacanth is a cryptid?" asked Miranda. "An un-discovered animal?"

"Precisely," he said. "Or at least it *was* a cryptid until main-stream scientists gave it their blessing. Coelacanths are still quite rare, but no longer the stuff of legends. Of course, your brother will be able to tell you all about them very soon." He looked at Jake. "I hope you're a good swimmer, *mi hijo*. Lake Lola is quite deep."

"That's great," replied Jake, hoping he sounded braver than he felt. "The deeper the better."

He wasn't afraid of water, but the idea of being in the same lake with giant eels, fish big enough to scare away giant eels, and possibly even an extinct sea monster made his heart bounce around in his chest like a rubber ball.

Cazador turned to Miranda. "And you, *señorita,* will be working with Diana Equinox in the aviary. There is no person in the entire world who knows more about cryptid birds. I'll take you over there myself in a moment."

"That sounds great," she said. "I love birds. I'm not sure if they'll love me, though."

Cazador laughed. "I have no doubt they will. You obviously have a way with animals." He returned his attention to Jake. "Cormick will be here in a few minutes to begin your orientation. Do you have any questions before I go?"

"Just one," said Jake. "What is a Mongolian death worm? Bolo Young mentioned it to us earlier this morning."

The doctor's bushy eyebrows arranged themselves into a frown. "Professor Becker hired Mr. Young to update our security system," he said. "I am told that he is the best at what he does. However, he has *no* business discussing cryptids with tyros—particularly *that* cryptid." He turned to Miranda. "And now, *señorita,* shall I take you over to Ms. Equinox?"

As Miranda and Cazador headed for the exit, Jake thought: What kind of cryptid is so dangerous that even Cazador won't talk about it?

14

The Four Laws

For Jake, life at the Z.I.A. felt more like summer camp than a job. And that was fine with him.

As Cazador told him would be the case, Jake hung out most of the time at the aquarium with Cormick and two other keepers. One was a soft-spoken Japanese man named Kano Jigaro, who worked at a famous zoo in Okinawa before Cazador hired him. Kano knew everything about fish cryptids, from goblin sharks to the Untouchable Bathysphere fish. The other keeper's name was Brody LaRue. He ran the Remote Operated Vehicles that the Z.I.A. used for deep-sea expeditions. Brody came from Baton Rouge, Louisiana. He sounded like a French person faking a southern accent or vice versa. When Brody and Cormick worked together, Jake practically needed a translator.

Miranda spent most of her time with Ms. Equinox in the aviary learning everything about the bizarre birds at the zoo. When she had time, she also helped with the goldhorns and the other hoofed mammals.

They were both careful not to tell their mother too much about their new jobs. For example, Jake knew she wouldn't be happy to hear about him scuba diving in Lake Lola with giant eels and fish the size of midsize sedans. For her part, Miranda conveniently forgot to mention that she hand-fed the carnivorous, grouchy centricores as well as a few raptors that could bite off her arm if they wanted.

One morning, Cormick told them that they'd both be working that day with a keeper named Marcelle Bondoc. "You'll love her!" he said as they walked away. "She's a true peach, that one. She'll learn ye everything you ever wanted to know about those huge beasties of hers."

They found Marcelle near the ink monkey enclosure, pushing a wheelbarrow full of red apples. She was about their mother's age, with long black hair and a wide friendly face. "This morning, we'll be working with our emela-ntouka," she told them after introductions. "That's Swahili for 'elephant killer,' for your information. But we call her Flower."

They made their way across the compound to an enclosure almost twice the size of the others, encircled by high cement walls.

"There she is," said Marcelle proudly. "Flower is the only emela-ntouka in captivity. Next fall, Professor Becker is sending me back to the Congo to try to locate a mate for her."

A beast the size of a taxicab lay under a palm tree, dozing. When it heard them, it lifted up its head and looked sleepily in their direction. It seemed to be one part rhinoceros and one part elephant, with a single ivory horn the size of an extra-large traffic cone in the middle of its forehead. It had a long, heavy-looking tail. As the animal got to its feet and lumbered toward them, they saw it also had a beak-like mouth and a strange flat growth on its head that frilled-out like a shield. Its hide was a dark shade of green and looked tougher than leather. They felt the vibrations from its heavy footsteps.

"Good morning, Flower," said Marcelle in a sing-song voice. She grabbed a few apples out of the wheelbarrow and tossed them over the dry moat that encircled the enclosure. "Breakfast time!"

They watched as the animal slowly bent down to seize one of the apples in its toothless but sharp-looking mouth. "She's enormous!" exclaimed Miranda. "Why didn't anybody ever find one of these before? She's impossible to miss."

Marcelle grinned and nodded. "That's always the first question tyros ask," she replied. "The other one is: 'If cryptids exist, why haven't they been written about in books?' As far as Flower is concerned, the short answer to both of your questions is that the native Pygmy people did find emela-ntoukas. But Pygmies aren't exactly book-publishing types. Trust me— if a cryptid is still alive *and* undiscovered, there's a very good reason for it."

"Like what?" asked Jake.

"It has to do with the second law of cryptozoology," she said. They stared at her blankly. "Didn't Dr. Cazador or Professor Becker explain the four laws to you?" They shook their heads. She shrugged. "Oh, well. I guess they want me to do it." She threw a few more apples into the pen. "Cryptozoologists rely on four main principles when we investigate a mysterious attack or respond to a lead from one of our sources."

"You mean you go around the world finding mysterious animals?" interrupted Miranda. "So you're secret agents? That's so cool!"

"Thanks," said Marcelle. "But we're really more like scientists who happen to be very good at animal control. Anyway, most of our sources live in the country where the cryptid is located. Once we get close, we can use the crypticon, but it only works within a half mile or so. Mostly, we rely on intelligence gathering, training, and hard work."

"What's a crypticon?" asked Jake, thinking that being a cryptid hunter sounded a lot better than going to school all day. "Is it like a tracking device?"

"Exactly. It's a handheld computer that can locate and identify any known cryptid using DNA patterning and other bio signatures," she explained. "Cazador only made two. He said he wanted to reduce the risk of the crypticon ever reaching the public. Poachers would love to get their hands on the technology."

"So what are the four laws?" asked Miranda.

"The first law," said Marcelle, holding up her thumb. "Cryptids are experts at hiding. They don't *want* to be found. If they were easy to find, we would have discovered them years ago and they wouldn't be cryptids. Usually, it's easy for them to stay hidden because they live in remote parts of the world. We tracked down Flower here after searching for an entire year in the Likouala Swamp in the northern Congo. Let me tell you, that place ranks dead last on my list of the world's must-see vacation spots."

"The second law," she continued, holding up two fingers. "Cryptids vigorously defend their hiding places. They somehow know that without their secrecy, they would die out. That's why most of them are *very* anti-social. So when you hunt cryptids, you better expect a fight, especially from the nasty ones."

"Do they try to eat you when you find them?" asked Jake, half joking.

Marcelle nodded. "Eat, crush, drown, poison." She waved her hand as if it were no big deal. "Whatever. But most of them are like Flower here. They just avoid being found in the first place. You wouldn't know it but she's very shy and her coloration makes her almost impossible to spot in the remote swamps of Africa. Isn't that right, Flower?"

Upon hearing her name, the immense animal took a step forward, crushing one of the apples with her foot. Marcelle threw her some more fruit and Flower went back to her meal.

The keeper held up three fingers. "The third law—cryptids and people and don't mix. That's why a big part of our job at the Z.I.A. is keeping the existence of cryptids a secret. It's the reason we have to respond to legitimate cryptid sightings right away. It's also why Cazador never sells cryptids and never opens up the zoo to visitors."

Miranda frowned. "I still don't get it. Humans have explored almost every inch of the planet. How could we have overlooked so many species?"

"What's so hard to believe?" she asked. "Scientists tell us that there are still hundreds of undiscovered species in the world. New ones are being found every day. Many of them are insects, tree frogs, or tiny fish at the bottom of the ocean, but a few are genuine cryptids. For example, we think Flower here might be some kind of long-lost ceratopsian, which would make her a living dinosaur. "

Her cell phone made a pinging sound. She glanced at it. "Oh, sorry, guys. I have to go feed the minhocãos. They start tearing up their enclosure if I'm late."

"What's a minhocão?" asked Miranda.

Marcelle put on her sunglasses. "Imagine an earthworm the

size of python and you get the picture," she said. She dumped the rest of the apples into the enclosure. "Come back tomorrow and I'll introduce you to them." She snapped her fingers. "I almost forgot. Professor Becker asked me to tell you to wait for him here."

"Wait!" shouted Jake as she began to walk away. "You never told us the fourth law."

She glanced back at them. "Right. The fourth law is—the cryptid you *don't* see is the most dangerous one of all."

15

A Bad Case of Lizard Gas

After Marcelle left, they watched Flower do a search-and-destroy mission on the apples. The animal moved slowly, as if tired of holding up the towering horn on its head. Eventually, Dr. Cazador and Professor Becker appeared. They seemed to be in the middle of a heated discussion.

"The whole thing is quite puzzling to me, Markus," Cazador said. "The security problems must be with the cages and enclosures themselves. And yet Dembi and Tuan haven't found anything wrong with them. That makes me think something else is going on, perhaps something more sinister. That's why I told Bolo that we need more surveillance cameras and guards patrolling at night."

"And what did he say?" asked the professor.

"He told me to let him do his work!" he said. "He said our main issues are the security breaches in our computer network. As if the cryptids were escaping though the Internet!"

Becker frowned. "Bolo Young is certainly rough around the edges. Still, he came highly recommended by people you and I trust. If he says that fixing our computer network should be our top priority, perhaps we should believe him. In any case, he tells me he's almost done."

"I hope so, Markus," he said. "I want him gone from here as soon as the job's completed. Something about him rubs me the wrong way."

"I agree," replied the professor. "I'll inform him today that we require those security cameras installed immediately."

Cazador nodded. When he finally noticed Miranda and Jake, he smiled broadly. "Good morning to my favorite tyros!" he exclaimed. "I apologize that I haven't gotten to spend as much time with you this summer as I would have liked."

"That's OK, doctor," said Miranda. "It's been a great experience so far. We've learned a lot."

"Wonderful," he replied. "Markus tells me that you're seeing the Tatzelwurms today. I wish I could join you, but another crisis beckons. I hope you understand." He smiled again and then turned and headed back toward the command center.

"I see Marcelle passed along my message to you," said Becker pleasantly after Cazador left. "As the doctor mentioned, you will meet our tatzelwurms today. Jeffrey and Richter will tell you everything you need to know. I'm certain you'll enjoy these cryptids. They are quite magnificent."

His cell phone rang. He removed it from his pocket and looked at it. "It's my source in Ireland. I'm sure it's another dobhar-chú sighting. We need to replace the specimen that went missing last month. If you'll excuse me." He turned on his heel and walked in the direction of the administration buildings.

"Cazador seems really upset," said Miranda when they were alone. "I wonder why the cryptids keep disappearing."

"Who knows?" said Jake, shrugging. "At least they're not keeping Bolo around much longer. That guy gives me the creeps. Come on. Let's go find the tatzelwurms."

They found the main pathway and took a left. Soon they saw a wooden sign in front of one of the smaller brown buildings. It read:

Tatzelwurm - *Draco Montis*

Like the other animal pens, the tatzelwurm house consisted of a long hallway that ran from the glass-walled enclosure area in front to storage rooms and offices in back. Inside they saw two middle-aged keepers talking to each other. One was tall and thin, with lank, black hair and a pinched face that made him seem as if he'd just eaten a lemon. The other was short and overweight, with thick-framed glasses and a pony tail.

"Ah, the new tyros," said the tall man as they entered. "Richter and I were just finishing our staff meeting. My name is Jeffrey."

"Nice to meet you," said Miranda, looking around the room. "Professor Becker told us that you're going to show us the tatzelwurms."

Jake sniffed the air. It smelled of swamp water and rotten meat. "Gross," he said. "What is that awful odor?"

"That would be the tatzelwurms, of course," said Jeffrey. "They're kind of the skunks of the reptile world, but far more treacherous. See for yourselves."

Miranda and Jake peered through the oversized glass wall that divided the corridor from the exhibit area. At first, the pen appeared to be uninhabited. In the middle of the cage, they saw a round pool of water that bubbled over its edges into a trough below. Several sinewy trees twisted around the cage's perimeter. Each leaf on the tree was as large as a hand.

Windows in the roof allowed in sunlight.

After a few seconds, several green shapes scurried out from the underbrush. Jake thought they were snakes at first, but he soon realized that something was very un-snake-like about them. First, their faces had an almost feline shape, with what appeared to be whiskers or hairs growing from very cat-like noses. They were each about three feet long, with oval, angry red eyes. They even had black ears lying flat against the back of their heads. Their skin was a deep, jungle green with irregular splotches of white bordered by maroon. A fan of frills ran halfway down the length of their spines.

Miranda was first one to see why the tatzelwurms could definitely *not* be snakes. "Look, Jake. They have two legs. No back legs, only front ones. And check out those claws!"

As Jake knelt down to examine the creatures through the window, one of them scrambled over to him, pulling itself along with its two arms. He saw that each of its hands sported three sharp-looking claws. The tazelwurm hissed at him, opening its mouth to reveal dozens of sharp teeth. All the lizards appeared to be extremely irritated, like little dogs trying to act tough.

"They're kind of scary," said Miranda. "Why do they keep hissing at us? Are they trying to keep us away from their home?"

"Not exactly," replied Jeffrey. "They're trying to kill you. Tatzelwurms breathe forth venom in the form of an aerosol, which paralyzes their prey. It's like the worst burp you've ever smelled. That's why we have to wear gas masks before we go into the pen." He pointed to three masks hanging on hooks next to the entrance door.

"You can feed them if you'd like," added Richter. "I thnk we could let you do that. I mean, if you're not too scared."

"I'll do it," said Jake quickly. He might be a tyro, but he didn't want anyone thinking he was scared of a few lizards, even if they *did* exhale poisonous gas. "You should wait here, Miranda. I know reptiles aren't really your thing."

"That's the understatement of the year," she said, shuddering. "They're disgusting. Show me how it's done, Jake, and maybe I'll try it later. Be careful."

He looked over at Jeffrey. "What do I give them once I'm in there?"

Jeffrey pointed to a plastic container by the office door. "Empty out that box of mice and the tatzelwurms will do the rest. Don't get your fingers too close to their mouths. They enjoy fingers."

The keepers began to talk to each other again in low voices as Miranda helped Jake put on the rubber gas mask. The mask felt hot and uncomfortable. It reminded him of those obnoxious latex things he used to wear on Halloween. "Is this right?" he asked Jeffrey when he had the mask on.

The keeper looked at him. "Not quite. Let me just make one adjustment." He tugged at the hose that ran from the mask to the small oxygen canister. "There. Now you're ready to go. Just go in there slowly and don't panic when they rush you. They're not nearly as dangerous as they look."

Jake opened the enclosure door and walked into a small anteroom with the box of mice. He pushed open a second door and stepped into the enclosure. The lizards immediately scurried over to him, wriggling their bodies like snakes, dragging themselves forward with their claws. When one passed the paved area around the pool, Jake could hear the clicking of its claws on the cement. One of the lizards immediately tried to chew off his toes. Panic seized him for a moment, but it subsided when he realized that the heavy-duty boots that Cazador gave him were made for this purpose. All the lizards could do was drool on him.

If they start climbing up his legs, he knew he would do some serious lizard stomping, regardless of how rare they are.

He placed the box carefully on the ground and turned it over. A dozen or so white mice darted out in every direction. To his relief, the tatzelwurms promptly lost interest in his feet and tore after the doomed rodents. He watched one of the lizards finally corner a mouse against one of the walls. It opened its mouth and hissed. Almost immediately, the rodent went stiff and fell over on its side. Even before its body had stopped twitching, the lizard began swallowing it whole.

Man, thought Jake. Jeffrey wasn't kidding about the deadliness of tatzelwurm breath.

He turned around to see if Miranda had caught the grisly performance. To his surprise, the corridor was deserted. That's weird, he thought. Where did everyone go?

Suddenly, his vision began to grow blurry. His stomach felt queasy and his head began to swim. He sat down hard on the cement floor, almost turning a tatzelwurm into a reptile pancake. It skittered away, hissing at him furiously. "Miranda?" he said out loud, glancing at the window. His voice sounded slurred. "Where are you?"

His eyelids grew heavy and his breathing became shallower. His heart felt like huge bass drum beating slowly inside his chest. He knew he should open the cage door and leave, but he couldn't even raise his hand. He also had a powerful urge to take a nap.

Then the world went dark, silent, and cold.

16

A Zoo within a Zoo?

J ake dreamed of unicorns.

"So do they exist?" asked a girl in his dream.

"Certainly many people over the centuries thought they did," replied a man's voice. "The Bible mentions them. Ancient Greek historians wrote long treatises about them. The authors of medieval bestiaries were as convinced of the unicorn's existence as they were of lions and tigers."

"But they were all wrong," the girl said. There was a pause. "Right?"

"Perhaps," said the man. "Did you know that Leonardo da Vinci wrote an essay on how to capture a unicorn?"

"Really?"

"He wrote that only a young maiden—such as yourself, for instance—could calm the unicorn's wildness. Only after the animal had placed its head peacefully on the maiden's lap could the hunters slay it."

"*Slay it?* Why would they do that?"

"I don't know. Why? Are you planning on doing any unicorn hunting in the near future?"

"No, I guess not," she admitted. "So do they exist or not?"

"When you say 'unicorn', do you mean a beautiful white

horse with a single narrow horn in the middle of its forehead?"

"Yes."

"No, I've never found such a creature in my travels."

The girl sighed heavily. "I knew it. I *really* hoped they were real."

"I didn't say they weren't real," the man replied. "I only said that *I* have never found one. I've heard rumors that Prince Alaweed has a unicorn in one of his private zoos. However, the man is a notorious liar."

"Prince Alaweed? Is he a cryptid hunter, too?"

"Of a sort. His methods and motives differ greatly from mine. The point is, Miranda, don't give up hope. You may find your unicorn yet."

Miranda? thought Jake. He wasn't dreaming after all. He was listening to a bizarre conversation between Dr. Cazador and his nerdy, unicorn-loving sister.

He willed his eyes to open. It felt like prying apart metal doors that had rusted shut.

"The slumbering prince awakens," said Cazador. "There is no rush, *mi hijo.* The effects of tatzelwurm poisoning can be slow to wear off."

Jake peered up at the ceiling of an unfamiliar room. His throat felt parched and he thought his head might burst. Miranda and Cazador peered over him like two physicians examining a patient. His sister knelt down beside him and hugged him tightly.

"What's going on? Where am I?" he asked groggily.

"We're in Cazador's apartment in the glass tower," said Miranda. "It's on the floor above the command center. There was a rip in your oxygen mask and you breathed in tatzelwurm gas. You've been unconscious for two hours."

"My head hurts," he said, sitting up on the leather couch. The afternoon sunlight pouring in through the windows made him squint. "What happened? I looked around and everybody was gone."

"After you went in with the lizards, Jeffrey got an emergency call," she explained. "Then they just took off. When I tried to open the door to the cage, it was locked. Luckily, another keeper walked by and I asked him to get Cazador. When the doctor arrived, we opened the door and dragged you out." She started to cry. "I'm so sorry, Jake. I thought you were going to die for sure."

Watching his sister cry made him feel even worse than the lizard gas. "Don't worry about it, Miranda," he said. "You did the right thing. I just got a long nap."

Cazador shook his head. "At least you're *alive*. But it was inexcusable for Jeffrey and Richter to leave you alone with the tatzelwurms. Completely unacceptable."

"Then why did they do it?" asked Jake. "Where did they go?"

"When Markus and I confronted them, they told me that Alan had called them in to help him with our orang mawa Priya, whom he believed had gone into labor," he explained. "It turned out to be a false alarm. Regardless, no crisis warrants leaving a tyro alone with a dangerous cryptid. Markus and I will be discussing disciplinary actions against those two keepers later today. "

Jake leaned back against the couch and closed his eyes. He wanted to tell Cazador that he suspected that Jeffrey had messed around with his breathing line when he made the last-minute adjustment. But why would Jeffrey do that? He'd only seen him once or twice during the summer.

Then he had an even more disturbing thought. Did Feng use another keeper to get back at Miranda and Jake for sneaking into the Z.I.A.? For being hired? Was he trying to make them quit?

Before he could voice these concerns to Cazador, however, the old man pointed to the sandwiches on the table in front of him. "No more talking," he said. "Eat. It will be another hour before you regain your full strength."

Jake grabbed a sandwich from the tray. He decided to keep his conspiracy theories to himself for now. Instead, he asked another question that had been bugging him for days.

"Doctor, why do you bring dangerous cryptids such as the tatzelwurms to the zoo?" he asked. "Wouldn't it have been better to just round them up and drop them off a cliff or something? Or just let them stay unknown?"

Miranda stared at him, clearly appalled, but Cazador didn't seem offended. "You make a valid point," he said. "Fully grown tatzelwurm are hardly lovable, though with a properly functioning gas mask they're harmless enough. However, the Z.I.A.'s primary mission is to discover and protect as many of the remaining specimens of rare animals before they go extinct, including the not-so-nice ones." He paused. "But even we don't bring back *every* dangerous cryptid to the Z.I.A. Not anymore."

"What do you mean?" asked Miranda. "What do you do with the really bad ones?"

The doctor sighed and walked over to the window. He tugged at his long beard, staring out at the zoo. "I wanted to postpone this conversation for another month, if not indefi-nitely. After your run-in with the tatzelwurms, I see that we must discuss it now." He paused, gathering his words. "There is another zoo at the Z.I.A. It is a hidden zoo populated by the most dangerous cryptids in the world."

Miranda and Jake looked at each other, flabbergasted. Then they both started asking questions at once.

The doctor held up his hand. "I'm not going to tell you where it is, so don't bother asking," he said. "I'll just say that it's so well hidden even you two couldn't find it. We call it the Underzoo."

Jake's eyes widened with excitement. "A secret zoo within a secret zoo? Filled with even deadlier animals than the Z.I.A? That is so cool!"

"I thought it was fairly, uh, *cool* once myself," he admitted. "The underzoo was my most ambitious project by far. I spent millions transforming an old silver mine on my property into a secure, underground facility for the world's deadliest cryp-tids. I planned to open both zoos to scholars from around the world. I wanted everyone finally to know the truth about cryptids—the good, the bad, and the ugly."

"So what happened?" asked Miranda.

"The Underzoo became my greatest failure," he said. "With-in a year of completion, we completely lost control of the fa-cility. I overestimated my abilities—or else I underestimated those of the cryptids. They were too treacherous, too unpre-dictable. Several of my finest keepers—my best friends—were injured or killed trying to contain them. In desperation, I fi-nally shut the doors forever." He paused and sighed. "Today, the Underzoo is no longer a zoo. It's just a prison."

"So that means that the Mongolian death worm—" began Jake.

"—is in the Underzoo," he said. "I placed seven of them there. However, I doubt any are still alive. At least, I *hope* they're not."

"If the cryptids in the Underzoo are so evil," asked Miranda. "Why did you capture them in the first place? Like Jake said, why didn't you just get rid of them?"

"Most cryptids are delightful, such as squonks and ink monkeys," he explained. "Others can be quite dangerous, but only if one acts rashly. It took my failure with the Underzoo to realize that certain cryptids are unacceptably hazardous no matter how many precautions one takes." He shook his head. "But that's all in the past. These days, the Z.I.A.'s most important mission is locating the worst cryptids around the world before they can harm humans. The ones we can capture, we bring here to the Underzoo. Those that we can't, we neutralize."

Cazador's cell phone rang. "What's going on, Markus?" He listened, nodding his head. "Tell Dembi to find the net and the PNEU gun, six cartridges, and the large-animal stomach pump. I'll call Cormick to bring the fork lift with the flat-bed attachment. I'll meet you at the enclosure in two minutes."

He returned the phone to his pocket. "A leontophone has just escaped. Alan thinks it went into Chung-Mae's enclosure. If she's already eaten it, she'll die soon unless we act quickly. Can you let yourself out after you feel better?" Without waiting for an answer, Cazador rushed over to the elevator and pressed a button. It opened and he entered.

Then they were left by themselves in Cazador's apartment

with a dozen burning questions on the tips of their tongues and no one around to answer them.

17

DIVING LAKE LOLA

They hardly saw Cazador at all over the next few weeks, so their questions about the Underzoo remained unanswered. They learned that Jeffrey and Richter were suspended for two weeks for the tatzelwurm incident. Jake still suspected Feng was behind it somehow, but since he had no evidence other than the nasty looks Feng gave him every day, he kept his mouth shut. Besides, he was too busy at the zoo to worry anyway.

Jake's favorite part about being a tyro was diving in Lake Lola. However, the first time he tried it, he had to admit he felt a little scared. All right—he felt *a lot* scared.

That first experience in the lake with Cormick was unforgettable:

"All right, boy, time to dive the loch," the Scotsman had told him, handing him a mask, fins, a belt with weights on it, and an oxygen tank. "You'll be knowin' how to use these?"

"No, Cormick," he replied. "I would not *be knowin'* anything about scubadiving in a *loch*. I've barely even gone snorkeling in my life. I think I tried it once with the Boy Scouts when I was ten."

"Och!" exclaimed the Scot. "Well, there's nothing to it. Not drowning is half the battle. And try not to panic when something large swims past ye." He winked and let out a hearty laugh. "Now what you've got there is a full face mask. It's a wee bit different than your average scuba set-up. Put her on and I'll help ye with the tank."

The water in the lake felt cold at first, but Jake got used to it quickly thanks to the wetsuit. He put his head under the water and stared down. The lake was clearer than he thought it would be. He could see about ten feet in front of him. There were tendrils of lake weeds rising up from the shallow water near the dock. He could see little brown fish swimming a few feet below him.

He heard Cormick's voice in his ear as they swam away from shore. "We'll only go down about thirty feet today," said Cormick, turning on a handheld diving light. The light revealed a few larger fish. Maybe trout, thought Jake. "Just wait till ye see the boggin eels!"

"Sounds great," said Jake, who felt more than a little nervous about the giant eels, particularly if they were "boggin" ones—whatever that meant. "Wait—how am I hearing you?"

"It's the masks, lad." Cormick tapped his head with his finger. "The regulators are built into 'em. Means you can talk to each other. The doctor enjoys a good chat on his dives. Come to think of it, so do I!"

They swam deeper into the dark water. With the diving light, Jake could see ten feet ahead of him. He glanced up at the surface, which now seemed far above him.

"All right, lad," said Cormick. "This is where those eejit devils should be breemin'. If one of 'em gets too close to ye, just give it a good skelping."

"A skelping?" asked Jake.

"You know. A smack on the backside."

Jake was pretty sure that eels didn't *have* backsides, but he gave him a thumbs-up. He felt a knot in his stomach that was a mixture of fear and excitement. His eyes darted back and forth, scanning the water in front of him.

The first eel passed so close to his mask that for a moment he thought he'd gone blind. It took forever for the eel's thick body to move past him. A moment later, another swam between Cormick and him, its torpedo-like body slicing briskly through the water and out of sight. The eels had two small fins up by their head and silvery-gray bodies rippling with muscle. Sometimes, they opened their mouths as if they were talking to one another. One of the larger eels bumped into him, like a Great Dane playing tag. Soon there were more than a dozen of them moving in and out of the light like moths around a lamp.

Long, slimy, evil-looking moths with lots of saw-like teeth, thought Jake.

"Och!" grunted Cormick. "These are big 'uns! They're grander than anything you've fished out of the streams 'round here I bet, eh, Jake?"

"They look like they have a lot of teeth," replied Jake, trying to sound as casual as possible. "Do you ever get bitten?"

"Aye, the rascals will nip ye now and again," he said dismissively. "Dinna worry! It's hard for them to bite through the wetsuit. Remember the skelpin'!"

And then as quickly as the eels had appeared, they were gone.

"Where'd they go?" asked Jake, looking around the area of the water illuminated by the powerful light.

"Wait and see, lad," said Cormick, chuckling. "You're in for a real treat."

Jake wanted to ask him if it was Lola, but he held his tongue. He still firmly believed Cormick and the others were only joking with him about the zoo's alleged, extinct plesiosaur and he didn't want to seem like more of a tyro than he already did.

"Ah, here she comes!" exclaimed Cormick. "*There's* my bonnie lass."

Emerging slowly out of the darkness was the biggest fish Jake had ever seen. It stretched at least ten feet, almost as long as the eels, with a shovel-shaped mouth that looked like it could swallow a dog. As it swam into the light, the fish examined them with black eyes the size of tea cups. The fish had big, dragon-like scales that were golden around its head becoming as red as brick on the rest of its body. It had stubby fins in front and a long, gold and red fin that rippled like a flag along its back.

"What is *that?*" asked Jake. "It looks like a torpedo with wings."

"That, my lad, is an arapaima," said Cormick joyfully. "Great giant of a fish from Malaysia. Not a cryptid, precisely, but a few of 'em drowned some fishermen outside Kuala Lumpur a while back. We went and thinned out the school a bit. Of course, we had to take a few home with us. I'm glad we did because they make the ruddy eels completely *mental*." He reached out and stroked the long fish as it swam past. "This one is Juanita. You can tell by that scar by her back fin. Good morning, my wee lass!"

Nothing was wee about Juanita, thought Jake. She was a submarine with eyeballs.

Cormick glanced at his watch. "Time to get back to the surface. Unless you'd care to dive a bit deeper? Swatch about for Lola?"

Jake stared past the monster fish named Juanita into the darkness below. "You can't fool me about Lola, Cormick. I know she doesn't really exist. I might be a tyro, but I haven't totally lost my mind."

Cormick grinned. "Suit yourself. She's probably giving birth to a wee bairn as we speak. Up we go!"

In the weeks that followed, Jake went on a dozen dives in the lake and the indoor tank with Cormick. It gave him a thrill every time. He loved the initial cold snap of the water, the strange Arapaimas swimming up from the depths to see if they'd brought food, even the obnoxious eels. Jake helped with the weekly fish count, making sure their numbers were either constant or increasing. He liked diving in the tank, too. He fed the fish, cleaned the glass and the coral, and tried to avoid getting flattened by a flying-saucer-sized turtle called Aengus.

Cormick turned out to be the friendliest person he'd ever met, despite his occasional loud outbursts of Scottish swear words. He constantly joked with Jake and the other keepers, needling them in his thick brogue.

"How much money do you think Dr. Cazador has spent on the Z.I.A.?" Jake asked him after a dive. "Fifty million dollars? A hundred million?"

The Scotsman shrugged. "I dunno. Money's nothing to that man. He'd spend every dollar he has tracking down the great undiscovered creatures of the world. He loves 'em, he does."

"Not *all* of them," said Jake carefully. "Not the ones in the Underzoo."

Cormick eyed Jake warily. "Aye, that's true enough. Which is why we spend a bit o' time ridding the world of the bad ones. Not all God's creatures can be harmless blob fish, can they? Now let's get lunch before I die of hunger. I'm famished!"

Like every day at lunch, keepers and other staff in the cafeteria separated themselves into two groups. Jake and Miranda observed this on their first day at the zoo. On one side of the room were the keepers who worked more closely with Cazador, Dembi, and Cormick. On the other side sat those who were closer to Feng and Bolo. This seemed to be a much larger group. Cazador himself *never* ate in the cafeteria. Jake wondered if he even realized how divided his staff really was.

As they entered the cafeteria, Jake looked at Cormick. "Why don't you ever eat sit with them?" he asked, indicating the Feng side of the cafeteria.

Cormick shrugged. "I got no problem with the professor. But I've no use for that Bolo eejit. And that Feng is a nasty piece of work. He knows better than to hang about the aquarium, I'll tell ye that!"

Eejit, as Jake learned, was Scottish for "idiot."

"Which reminds me," continued Cormick. "Dembi, me, and six other keepers are flying to Kenya tomorrow on a special mission. You won't believe it, Jake. They actually found a nandi bear!" He waited breathlessly for a reaction, a goofy grin on his face.

"That's great, I guess," Jake replied at last. "What the heck is a nandi bear? It sounds like a candy."

Cormick shook his head. "That's a laugh! This kind of a candy will chew on *you*! No, the nandi bear is a nasty creature, a ferocious carnivore—cranky as a one-eyed badger. It has great, high shoulders and a sloping back. From head to toe it's taller than a Grizzly. It can ruin a cow with one swipe of its claws. We've heard reports for years, mostly out of western Kenya. There's usually evidence of massive cranial trauma in the victims."

"Cranial trauma?" asked Jake. "What do you mean?"

The Scotsman winked. "The muckle bear likes to eat their brains."

Jake winced. "OK. I have to admit that sounds kind of awesome and scary at the same time. So you're going there to catch it?"

He nodded. "Or kill it. It's been terrorizing villages, taking livestock, and the like. Professor Becker already stocked the jet with equipment and provisions. We're all set to go."

"That's great," said Jake weakly. "Well, be careful. Don't let it eat your brain—you might need it later." He paused. "I don't know what I'm going to do around here while you're gone."

Cormick patted him on the back. "Not to worry, lad. We'll be back in a wink. There'll be gobs of time for more dives in the loch." He looked at him seriously for a moment. "Besides, I need you and your sister to keep an eye on the doctor. I'm worried about him. He hasn't been himself lately. He stays up in that tower more and more these days. He misses his adventures, I reckon. Take care of him for us, will ye?"

"We'll do our best," replied Jake. "Happy hunting in Kenya."

They said good-bye and Jake put two plates of food onto a tray. Then he left the cafeteria and made his way down to the aviary.

13

The Cryptid Thief

The aviary was almost as large as the aquarium, with high nets instead of walls. Birds were divided into separate areas by more netting. A brick pathway meandered through it, ending at a stone table in the center.

Jake found his sister sitting at a bench with her favorite animal (besides Pablo) at the zoo. The violet-colored bird paid him no attention at all as he sat down at the table. It sat perched on a metal stand next to the bench, its soft eyes staring serenely into space. It seemed to be a hundred different shades of purple, with long tail feathers that reached twice its length. An area of dark, plum-colored wing feathers made it appear as if it had purple gloves on. A dozen or so long plumes of white-fringed feathers on its head stretched behind it like hair. The bird sat placidly on its perch, enjoying every bit of the attention Miranda was giving it.

"Hi, Jake," said Miranda cheerfully. "I'm helping Portia with her preening. She's such a spoiled girl, even for a Purple Bird of Paradise. Aren't you, Portia?"

The bird made several pleasant cooing sounds as Miranda rubbed its back and head, occasionally removing a stray feather. After a minute, she picked up the bird gently in her arms and carried it over to a door in one of the large netted areas.

She opened the door and released the bird. Then she washed her hands at an outdoor sink.

"The choices were grilled salmon or ostrich burgers," said Jake, who had already started eating. "I figured you'd want the fish."

Miranda sat down with him at the table. "Ostrich burgers?" she exclaimed, making a disgusted face. "That sounds horrible! Who would eat an ostrich?"

"I don't know," he said. He took a bite of the bird burger. A little dry, but otherwise pretty good. "Everybody? Ostriches are annoying."

"I bet they think *you're* annoying," she said with a grin. "Speaking of dumb birds, that oozlum I told you about still keeps bumping into the other birds. He's going to hurt himself one of these days. We're trying to teach him to fly forward, but how are we supposed to do that? He admires his own tail feathers too much and he can't see them if he's flying forward, can he?"

Jake took a bite of his apple. He had grown used to these bizarre conversations with his sister. The cryptids they'd worked with that summer often defied explanation. He peeked down at Miranda's electronic notebook on the table. There were brief descriptions of some of the birds she cared for:

Cinnamon Bird:
Also known as cinnamologus or cinnibird. It kind of resembles a golden eagle, but it smells like Grandma Jinks' apple pie. Huge bird from Saudi Arabia region that collects cinnamon to build its nests.

Devil Bird:
Captured in Sri Lanka by Dembi. Also known as an ulama. It's like the weirdest looking owl you've ever seen. Its eyebrows stick out two inches on either side of its head! Its shriek is not funny, though. It makes a sound like a person getting chased by zombies. Equinox moved all the Devil Birds into sound-proof cages after Cazador complained that they were interrupting his naps. I wear ear plugs when I visit them.

Ngoima:
Bird from the Congo with a wing span of 13 feet. It sort of resembles a crow in the way a kitten resembles a lion. Scary. Eats an entire goat every day! Super gross. Keepers have to wear a catcher's mask and other protective gear when they feed it.

Caladrius:
Snowy white bird from Egypt. Seems pretty normal in appearance, like an egret. Won't look at a person if it thinks that person will die soon. And it always knows! Mrs. Equinox told me that it once avoided eye contact with a keeper for an entire week. That weekend, the keeper died of a heart attack. Spooky. Luckily, the Caladrius has no problem looking at me.

Shang Yang:
Single-legged bird from China. A very beautiful crane that is mostly white except for the black feathers around its head and wing tips. It's almost as tall as I am when it stands. It's name means the "bird that makes the rain." Hops and flaps its wings when rain is in the forecast. Equinox says it's never wrong.

As they ate their lunch, Jake told her about his conversation with Cormick regarding the brain-eating nandi bear expedition.

"Well, I guess finding that bear must be worth it," said Miranda. "Otherwise Dr. Cazador wouldn't let them go. He'd want them to stay and complete the new security overhaul." She paused. "So Cormick still hasn't told you anything about the Underzoo?"

"Not a word. There must be some really amazing cryptids down there if no one will even *talk* to us about it. I wonder if they'll bring the bear back and put it in the Underzoo."

She shuddered. "I hope not. Oh, that reminds me. I need to tell you something." She glanced over her shoulder to make sure no one was around. "You know that cryptids have been disappearing from the zoo, right?"

"Of course," he replied. "They keep escaping from their enclosures. It's why Professor Becker hired Bolo."

She leaned in close. "What if they're *not* escaping?" she whispered. "What if someone is *stealing* them?"

He frowned. "What are you talking about?"

"Remember a few weeks ago when we were up in Cazador's tower?"

"How could I forget?" he replied. "That was the day those stupid tatzelwurms gassed me."

"Do you remember Cazador getting an emergency call about Chung-Mae eating the leontophone?"

He nodded. "I remember. He left us up in the tower. Mom got mad at us because we didn't get home until eight."

"Right. Anyway, Chung-Mae turned out to be fine. Maybe she ate it and it had no effect or maybe the leontophone got away. Either way, they never found it."

"What's your point? It probably just ran off or some hawk got it."

She glanced nervously around the aviary again. "I don't think so. I had some free time this morning, so I was reading by Flower's enclosure. I overheard Alan Feng talking to someone on his cell phone. He didn't see me. He kept mentioning something about delivering a rat and getting his money. I think he was negotiating with somebody." She paused, staring at him. "Don't you get it? I don't think the leontophone escaped at all. I think Feng *stole* it and pretended that it escaped."

Jake put down his burger. "You're saying Feng made up the story about Chung-Mae eating the leontophone so that he could *sell* it?"

"Shh!" she said, looking around. "Yes, that's exactly what I'm saying."

"It seems a little far-fetched to me. I mean, why would you steal a leontophone? How much could one be worth anyway?"

"I heard Feng mention $20,000."

Jake whistled. "That's a lot of money for a rodent." He thought about it for a second. "It doesn't shock me that Feng's a thief, but we need more proof before we can say anything to Cazador or Professor Becker. Right now, it's just our word against Feng's."

She nodded excitedly. "That's the other thing I wanted to tell you! Feng told the person on the phone that he'll meet him tonight at the Owl Cafe. Isn't that a restaurant in Ranchita?"

He grinned. "I see where you're going with this. We can get Mom to take us to dinner tonight and catch Feng in the act."

"Exactly," she said. "If we can do it without him knowing

we're there, we'll have all the information we need to get him in big, big trouble."

He got up from the table. "Let's do it," he said. "I've got to get back to the aquarium. See you at four."

He hustled toward the aviary exit. If they could catch Feng selling a cryptid, Dr. Cazador and the professor would *have* to fire him. And the Z.I.A. without Alan Feng would make their lives much easier. And *safer.*

They cornered their mother when she got home from work. They told her that they wanted to eat at the Owl Cafe because so many people at the Z.I.A. went there. This wasn't exactly true, but it wasn't quite a lie, either. At least Alan Feng must like it, since he chose it for his illegal rendezvous.

"What a wonderful idea!" exclaimed their mother. "We haven't gotten to spend much time together this summer. You can tell me how your job at the zoo is going."

By six o'clock, they were sitting inside the restaurant, which consisted of several dark rooms with cramped wooden booths and fake leather cushions. It had an old-fashioned wooden bar that had probably been there since Billy the Kid rode to town. Only about ten people were in the restaurant. None of them appeared to be Feng.

Jake looked down at the menu. It featured a mix of Mexican and American food, which seemed to be typical of every restaurant in Ranchita. At least they had green-chile cheeseburgers, he thought. With the exception of the Z.I.A, green-chile cheeseburgers were the best things about New Mexico.

"So tell me everything about your internships," said their mother after they had ordered dinner. "Or I guess they're called tyroships, aren't they?"

"It's been really fun, Mom," said Miranda. "The Z.I.A. is so much better than the National Zoo. The animals are a lot more, um..." She hesitated. "Interesting. Right, Jake?

"Definitely," he said. "We're learning a lot from the other keepers. All of them are experts in their field from all over the world. And most of them are really cool."

They did not need to scare their mother with stories of 15-foot lake eels, sheep-eating birds, or poison-burping lizards.

Or an alleged cryptid thief that might walk through the door any minute.

Jake scanned the restaurant again. Every person appeared to be a local. There were farmers, older couples, and a few young families. Feng could have arrived earlier, he thought. Or maybe he was coming later. Or maybe they were just wrong about the leontophone. He looked over at Miranda, who couldn't hide her disappointment.

When they were finished, their mother paid the bill and they got up to leave. It was dark outside as they walked to the car.

"Sorry, Jake," Miranda whispered. "I thought he'd be here for sure."

"At least we tried," he replied. "And my burger was good."

They were about to get into their car when a white pick-up truck raced into the parking lot. Jake tapped Miranda on the shoulder. "It's him!"

Feng pulled his truck into a nearby parking space, chatting obliviously on his cell phone. Jake knew that once the keeper got out of the car, he'd look up and see them. Suddenly, confronting a possible cryptid thief with no one from the Z.I.A. to help them seemed like a bad idea.

123

"Could you please open the door, Mom?" Jake asked urgently. "I'm dying to get home. I'm exhausted."

"Of course," she said, fumbling with her keys. She looked up and saw Feng's truck. "Isn't that one of the keepers from your zoo? I think I met him when I visited the zoo that time. It would be rude of us to run off without saying hello."

Before they could stop her, she walked over to the truck just as Feng got out. In his right hand, he carried a small cage covered in a cloth. It looked big enough to carry a small dog.

Or a $20,000 lion-killing mouse, thought Jake.

"Good evening," said their mother warmly, holding out her hand. "I'm Samantha Jinks. I'm Jake and Miranda's mother. You're Mr. Feng, right? We met briefly at the Z.I.A. last month."

Stunned, Feng glanced from their mother to them. Jake knew they looked as shocked as he did. Feng shook their mother's hand limply, trying unsuccessfully to hide the cage behind his back.

"Oh, hello," he mumbled. "What are all of you doing here?"

Since there was no use pretending they weren't there any more, thought Jake, they might as well see what he is up to.

"We just had dinner. Great food here. I recommend the green chile cheeseburgers. By the way, what have you got there? Is that an animal carrier?"

Their mother finally noticed that Feng was holding the container. "How nice! Did you bring your dog to eat with you? You must be quite attached. What breed is it?"

Feng's face was now a blotchy mix of anger and panic. For a moment, Jake thought that he was going to jump back in the truck and speed away. "It's not a dog," he blurted out at last. "I mean, my dog is resting right now. Now if you'll excuse me, I really must—"

"Couldn't we just have one little peek at your dog, Mr. Feng?" asked Miranda innocently. "You know how much we *love* animals. What's its name?"

"That's no concern of yours!" shouted Feng, visibly upset now. "If you don't mind, I must go have my dinner." He shot them a nasty look and practically sprinted across the parking lot to the restaurant.

Their mother frowned. "What an unpleasant man," she said. "I certainly hope the other zookeepers aren't like him."

"No, most of them are nice," said Miranda. "Alan Feng is unique."

"That's one way of putting it," she replied. "He's uniquely awful."

"Don't worry, Mom," said Jake, exchanging a look with Miranda. "We sort of doubt Feng will be working at the zoo much longer."

"That's probably a good thing," she replied. "There's something about him that doesn't add up. It was as if we had caught him robbing a bank or something. He acted so guiltily."

He sure did, thought Jake. And tomorrow, he and Miranda would make certain that Dr. Cazador and Professor Becker knew *exactly* how guilty Feng really was.

19

The Secret Book of Beasts

As they rode their bikes to the zoo the next morning, they strategized about how they would tell the others about Feng.

"I think we should go directly to Professor Becker," said Miranda. "He'll know what to do. We can stop by his office before we even go to our jobs. "

"I don't know," replied Jake. "Shouldn't we speak to Cazador first? He's the owner of the Z.I.A., after all."

"But we haven't even seen him in two weeks!" she said. "He's always in his tower. I'm worried that we won't be able to find him before we run into Feng."

"I'm hoping Feng doesn't even show up today," said Jake. "I guess we can just play it by ear."

When they got to the gate, Jake punched in the code and it opened. Unlike every time before, however, no one was waiting to meet them.

"That's weird," said Miranda. "I guess we're biking a little farther today."

After five more minutes on their bikes, they got to the hill overlooking the compound. To their suprise, pricey-looking cars and limousines filled the normally half-empty employee parking lot.

"What are all these fancy cars doing here?" asked Jake, slowing his bike down. "Did all the keepers get raises? Maybe we can get new bikes. Or motorcycles!"

"In your dreams," replied Miranda. "Anyway, there's no way those cars belong to keepers. They're too nice. There's something going on that we don't know about."

He frowned. "Maybe you should go with me to the aquarium this morning until we find out what's going on."

"Good idea," she said. "Lead the way, fish boy."

They rode their bikes through the zoo until they were in front of the aquarium. As they were about to enter the building, Jake spotted Feng by the Maltese tiger enclosure. He was talking to an extremely fat man in an expensive suit and puffing on a cigar. Next to them were three large men wearing dark glasses and bulky leather jackets.

"Oh, no," said Jake. "Feng showed up. And he brought some friends."

"I don't think Feng has friends," replied Miranda. "Those look like bodyguards to me."

Feng gestured toward Chung-Mae's enclosure, explaining something to the man in the suit, who nodded and blew smoke into the air. Luckily, no one was facing their direction.

"I have a strange feeling that something bad is going on," said Miranda nervously. "We better go inside before Feng sees us."

Inside, they were greeted by more weirdness. At least two dozen people milled around the central tank and the other enclosures. For a moment, Jake wondered if the Z.I.A. had suddenly been opened to the public. But the visitors didn't didn't act like tourists. There were no crying kids begging for ice cream. Nobody wore flip-flops or Hawaiian shirts. Instead, the room teemed with well-dressed executive-types holding clipboards and taking notes. Most of them were being escorted around by keepers in Z.I.A. uniforms. Jake saw Jeffrey, the keeper who had probably sabotaged his oxygen mask in the tatzelwurm enclosure. Richter stood next to him, speaking with a small group of people.

What was going on? Jake wondered. Did only keepers who hated them come to work today?

Miranda pointed toward the salamander exhibit. "There's Tuan," she said. The keeper stood all by himself, gazing forlornly around the aquarium. "He'll be able to tell us what's going on. Let's talk to him."

They walked over to him. "What's up, Tuan?" said Jake. "What are all these people doing here? When did Dr. Cazador start letting in the general public to the Z.I.A.?"

"I don't know," he said, his eyes darting nervously from them to the visitors. "I was feeding the salamanders and then everyone showed up at once. Jeffrey told me that Dr. Cazador approved it, but I don't believe him."

"Approved what?" asked Miranda. "Tours?"

"Sales!" exclaimed Tuan. "He says Cazador is selling all the cryptids and closing down the Z.I.A."

Jake stared at him in disbelief. "That's crazy!" he said. "Have you spoken to Cazador today? And where's Professor Becker?"

He shook his head, clearly distraught. "I haven't seen either of them. Alan is in charge."

Miranda caught Jake's eye. He knew what she was thinking because he thought the same thing: Stealing the leontophone and the other missing cryptids had been the tip of the iceberg for Feng. His real goal is to take over the Z.I.A.!

"I almost forgot!" exclaimed Tuan. He reached into his bag and pulled out a package wrapped in brown paper. It had the name "Jinks" hastily scrawled on it in black marker. "I found this in my locker this morning. I don't know who put it there, but whoever it is wanted you to have it."

"Thanks," replied Jake, taking it from him. "What are you going to do now?"

He glanced around worriedly. "I'm going home. It's not safe here. You should come with me."

"Not yet," Miranda replied. "Jake and I want to make sure the professor and Cazador are all right. Then we'll leave."

"Be careful," said Tuan uneasily. "A lot of these guys have guns and you can be sure they know how to use them."

They left Tuan standing by the salamander enclosure with his half-empty bucket of fish. Just before they reached the exit, Jeffrey spotted them and ran over to them.

"You're not supposed to be here," he snapped. "I sent emails and texts to everyone. Essential staff only."

"Well, I guess we didn't get the memo," said Jake, annoyed. "Where are Dr. Cazador and Professor Becker? What has Feng done with them?"

The keeper seemed taken aback for a moment. "I don't know what you're talking about," he stammered. "And it doesn't matter anyway. Cazador is shutting down the Z.I.A. All the cryptids are being sold."

"Dr. Cazador loves this zoo," said Miranda. "He would never close it down. And he *definitely* wouldn't sell any cryptids. That's a violation of one of the four laws."

Jeffrey smirked. "Cazador made the laws so I guess he can

break them if he wants to. If I were you, I'd get back on your bikes and leave the Z.I.A. as fast as you can. If Alan finds out you're here..." His voice trailed off and he turned abruptly and went back to the group by the tank.

Miranda was trembling with anger. "This can't be happening! Why would Cazador sell the Z.I.A. right now?"

Jake thought about it. "Don't you think it's a weird coincidence that this is happening on the *exact* weekend that most of the keepers left for Africa?" he said. "I think Feng waited until everyone was out of the way to make his move."

Jeffrey was now speaking furiously into his cell phone, his eyes fixed on them like lasers. Two of the large men standing next to him glanced over at them with fierce looks.

"Let's get out of here," said Miranda. "We can use one of the side exits. We need to find out what's in this package and why someone left it for us. Hurry!"

They walked quickly past the cryptid shoppers and the central tank to the side door. When they were outside, they tore open the paper wrapping. Inside was a thick, leather-bound book. The cover was tattered and worn, with dark stains on the edges of the pages that looked like dried blood. In neat gold script on the book's cover it read:

:: Underzoo Bestiary ::
Property of Dr. J.S.L. Cazador
Do Not Remove From Premises.
TOP SECRET!

20

Betrayed!

They leafed quickly through the pages of the Bestiary. The book contained the names, descriptions, and photos of every animal in the Underzoo. Next to each entry was information about where and when a cryptid was found, who was on the capture team, drawings, photographs, and a list of the animal's physical features. Not surprisingly, they were unfamiliar with most of the cryptids: amaroks, chupacabras, culebróns, water tigers, mahambas, and something called a yacumama.

It was like a yearbook of the world's worst animals, Jake thought. If hell had its own collection of animals, they'd all be in the Underzoo.

"These cryptids make tatzelwurms seem like class pets," remarked Miranda. She turned to Jake. "Who do you think left this book for us?"

Jake felt a shiver of fear race down his spine. "I don't know," he replied. "But we need to find out soon. I have a feeling it has a lot to do with the new guests."

They stuffed the book into Miranda's backpack and made their way over to the glass tower. The cool morning had given way to the heat of the day. As they passed by the animal pens, they noticed that several were empty, their front doors wide open. When they went by the squonk enclosure, three of the animals cowered in the back of their pen, thick tears cascading down their warty faces. Squonks weren't brave even in the best of circumstances, but now they were terrified.

"One of them must have already been sold," said Jake. "Who would buy a squonk? They're totally useless."

"They're cryptids, Jake," Miranda replied impatiently. "A white lion cub is worth $100,000 and it's not even endangered. Who knows what a squonk might be worth?"

They saw several more keepers touring buyers around the zoo. There also seemed to be more of the men in black uniforms with automatic rifles. They stopped at a building next to the tower. Two muscle-bound men stood on either side of the tower's entrance. They were dressed in black and wore black baseball hats. They stared coolly out at the people in the compound through their reflective sunglasses, their holstered guns making their jackets bulge.

"That must be where Cazador and Professor Becker are being held prisoners," said Jake. "We need to figure out a way to get up there."

"But how can we get to the elevator?" asked Miranda. "Those guys aren't going to let us just walk in."

Jake thought about it. "I know how to get rid of them."

She eyed him skeptically. "You're not going to do anything stupid, are you?"

"Only a little stupid." He grinned. "Trust me. I'll be right back."

He raced back to the squonk enclosure, typed in the code, and opened the door. The squonks peered up at him mournfully from their blood-shot eyes. "Good morning, piggies!" he announced. "Who wants some exercise?"

He herded the squonks out the door towards the tower. "Here goes nothing," he mumbled. "All right, boys and girls. It's time for some exercise!"

With his hand, he smacked one of the animals on its rear end. The squonks took off down the path toward the tower like chubby cruise missiles. They flew directly past the guards by the tower gate with Jake close behind them. He halted in front of the guards.

"You have to help me!" he said, leaning over and panting as if exhausted. "Those squonks are worth $50,000 bucks each. Don't just stand there. Do something!"

The guards watched in alarm as the creatures tore down the zoo's main path up the hill. They glanced at Jake's uniform and name tag. As he'd hoped, the men assumed he was just another clueless keeper. They started loosening their ties. "How do we catch 'em?" asked the taller one.

Jake pretended to think about it for a second. "Easy. All you have to do is to tickle them gently on their belly. Once you do that, they flop right over and take a nap."

The two men nodded. "You're sure that's all we have to do?"

Jake nodded. "It works every time. Hurry! They're heading up the hill toward the gate!"

They turned and sprinted after the fleeing squonks like the football linebackers they probably once were. In a minute, Miranda emerged from the other side of the tower.

"Very impressive," she said. "So *that's* what pulling off a successful prank feels like."

Jake grinned. "At least this time it's for a good cause. Now let's go rescue the professor and Cazador."

They pushed open the gate and ran to the elevator. In less than a minute, they stepped out of the elevator into the command center.

It was like a tornado had ripped through the place. Books and papers were everywhere. The computers were gone, their flat-screen terminals face down on the floor. The room seemed to be abandoned, except for a person hunched in an armchair near one of the tall windows.

It was Cazador. He looked terrible. His white hair was unkempt and his white suit was wrinkled and dirty. There was a dark bruise on his left check. It didn't appear that he had slept for days. When he saw them, he pushed himself stiffly up from his chair with his black staff. Pablo, who had been curled in a ball next to him on the couch, scrambled over to Miranda.

"My brave tyros!" he exclaimed. "You're the first friendly faces I've seen in two days." His face suddenly went rigid with fear. "But you shouldn't be here! You're in grave danger."

"Are you OK, Dr. Cazador?" asked Jake. "What's going on? Are you really selling the Z.I.A.?"

"Certainly not!" he said indignantly, his eyes wild and intense. "I've been betrayed. We've *all* been betrayed. You must leave the zoo at once while you still can."

"We know it's Feng," said Miranda quickly. "We should have called you when we found out two days ago. I heard him talking about selling the leontophone and then we caught him in the act on Friday night at the Owl Cafe. We think he might be responsible for all the missing cryptids. If we had known that he would try to take over the zoo—"

"You don't understand," interrupted Cazador. "Alan *is* involved, but he's not shrewd enough to have done this all by himself. He needed someone powerful, someone with connections to—"

Suddenly, the elevator door opened and Feng and Bolo Young stepped into the room. They were followed closely by Professor Becker.

"How lovely for you, Cazador!" exclaimed the pale director, a thin trace of a grin on his face. "Your rescuers have arrived at last." He shook his head, almost sympathetically. "But I'm afraid this is a classic case of too little and much, much too late."

21

Villains Victorious

Professor Becker stared at them triumphantly. Alan Feng stood next to him, grinning as though he'd just won the lottery. Behind them stood Bolo, smirking like a hyena, his eyes hidden behind his mirrored sunglasses. All three men now carried pistols on their hips.

"What a *fool* I've been," muttered Cazador bitterly. "You've been planning this for years, haven't you, Markus? You hired Alan, Bolo, Jeffrey—how many more?—all with this coup d'état in mind. You're diabolical."

"I'll take that as a compliment," replied the professor. "It certainly took you long enough to catch on. I assume you've guessed the name of my benefactor?"

"Only one person has the resources to finance all this," replied the doctor. "Alaweed."

"Are Miranda and I the only ones in this room who don't know who that is?" interrupted Jake.

Cazador kept his eyes fixed on Becker. "Prince Alaweed is the most notorious exotic animal collector in the world. He's greedy, cunning, and ruthless. He's always coveted the Z.I.A., but I never dreamed he'd engineer a takeover using my own people as his puppets."

"I'm hardly a puppet," said Becker indignantly. "All of this is the result of my formidable intelligence and skill. Alaweed did loan me Bolo so that I could speed the process along. In less than a week, we hacked your accounts, fired all the keepers loyal to you, and arranged the auction of your cryptids. And we did it all right under your nose." He met the doctor's gaze with his lifeless, blue eyes. "In point of fact," he continued, touching his tongue to his upper lip like a reptile. "You're *my* puppet, Cazador. I can make you dance, sing—or I can cut your strings altogether."

The doctor shook his head. "We've known each other for ten years, Markus," he said, his voice rising. "I hired you when no other zoo would even take your call. I gave you the opportunity to find the rarest animals in the world. And *this* is how you repay me? By sending my keepers off on some phony mission so that you can hand over the zoo to a villain?"

Professor Becker curled his lip into a sneer. "If you had been *half* the cryptozoologist you once were, I couldn't have done it. I knew you and Cormick wouldn't be able to resist the prospect of catching a nandi bear. So I paid your source in Kenya an ungodly amount to make up his little story. That means Cormick, Dembi and the rest of them won't be back in satellite communication for another week. You're on your own."

"Being a backstabbing traitor is hardly something to brag about," interrupted Miranda. She held Pablo in her arms, the monkey's wise oval eyes peering out of its blue mask. "You'll never get away with this."

Becker turned his gaze at her as if seeing her for the first time. "This isn't some kind of Hollywood action film, girl," he said coldly. "And in case you haven't been paying attention, I've *already* gotten away with it."

"But why, Markus?" asked Cazador, putting his arm around Miranda. "You helped build this zoo. Why throw it all away?"

Becker gazed down at the compound as a forklift loaded a cage with three squonks in it onto the back of pickup truck. "I had a revelation recently, Cazador," he said. "I discovered that I don't like animals, cryptid and otherwise. I don't enjoy seeing them. I don't enjoy feeding them. I certainly don't enjoy smelling them. What I *do* enjoy is money. It so happens that Alaweed has piles and piles of it, which he'll give to me if I give him the Z.I.A."

"The professor and I will be hunting cryptids for him now," interjected Feng with undisguised glee. "With the prince's black market connections and our cryptid hunting skills, who knows? We might become as rich as you, Cazador." He smirked. "As rich as you *were,* anyway."

The professor shot an icy glance at Feng. "You're fortunate the prince didn't feed you to his goblin sharks, Alan," he said. "It was stupid of you to steal those cryptids before we could take over the zoo. We had to accelerate our plans as a result. You nearly ruined everything."

Feng looked hurt. "What did a few missing cryptids matter? The prince would never have missed them. And I needed the cash!"

The professor rolled his eyes. "It doesn't matter now. The real money is in this." He took out what seemed to be a tablet or oversized cell phone from his pocket. "Once the prince reverse engineers your little invention for the world market, we'll make millions."

Jake looked at Miranda. Although neither of them had ever seen the device before, they knew immediately what it must be. It was the crypticon.

"*Malvado!*" shouted Cazador, waving his black cane. "Giving the crypticon to Alaweed would guarantee the disappearance of every cryptid in the world! Have you lost your mind?"

Becker returned the device to his jacket pocket. "Your quaint vision of saving exotic animals is outdated, Cazador. Will anyone besides you shed a tear if every orang mawa on the planet goes extinct? Who cares if a pack of amaroks eats a few natives in some godforsaken arctic village? It's about time someone put your crypticon to good use."

The doctor turned pale. His mouth opened again, but no words came out this time.

"Splendid!" exclaimed the professor. "I've finally rendered the great Cazador speechless." He turned to Jake and Miranda, placing a slender finger against his lips. "Now for your protégés—whatever shall we do with *you?*"

"Keep them out of this," Cazador growled. "You've got what you want. Let them go. I give you my word they won't say anything to the authorities."

Becker's eyebrows shot up in mock surprise. "Did you hear that, Bolo? They won't report us to the authorities! I feel so much safer now."

Miranda took a step forward. "If we aren't home when our mom gets back from work today, she'll go to the police," she said. "Then the police will come here."

"I certainly hope so," he replied smugly. "In fact, I'm counting on it. After all, I'll need to explain to your worried mother and the Ranchita Police exactly what happened." He paused. "I'll give them the flight log showing that all three of you went to Kenya with the other keepers. I'll hand over the letter that you wrote to your mother—forged of course—telling her you'll be back in a week."

Cazador's face became ashen. "You wouldn't!"

"Oh, but I *would*," said the professor, sneering at him. "I'll tell them I begged you not to take the children with you, but that you were too stubborn—or maybe too demented—to listen. When Dembi and the others return next week, the FBI will be waiting for them. Meanwhile, Bolo, Feng, and I will be gone, along with the crypticon and every animal worth selling at this freak-show of a zoo."

The doctor sat down heavily on the couch. He appeared to be too stunned to speak.

Jake glared at Becker. "Since we're obviously not in Kenya, what are you really going to do with us? Lock us up in a dungeon or something?"

The professor studied him like a bakeneko sizing up a mouse. "Not a dungeon, exactly, but you're *so* close." He looked over at Cazador, who stared blankly at the floor. "I wonder where I might hide someone if I wanted to make sure that person would never, ever, *ever* be found again? Do you have any ideas, Cazador?"

The doctor looked up at Becker, loathing in his eyes.

"Enough chit-chat," said the professor abruptly. "Let's go for a stroll, shall we?"

22

Burying the Evidence

As they stepped into the courtyard, Jake shielded his eyes against the blinding midday sun. The security guards he had sent on the wild squonk chase were again at their posts by the entrance gate to the tower. One of them clutched a pair of broken sunglasses. Both appeared to have just run a marathon. They didn't look happy to see him.

"I hope you guys had a good jog," said Jake. "I guess the squonks won, huh? How did that tickling thing work out?"

They marched in single file toward the lake behind Becker and his men. Armed people in black uniforms were everywhere, busily removing the cryptids from their enclosures.

Becker has his own private army now, thought Jake. Or maybe Prince Alaweed loaned him one. Either way, they had conquered Cazador's kingdom without even firing a shot. He looked at Miranda, who was walking a few feet in front of him. "How are you doing?" he asked.

"I'm fine," she said under her breath. "Actually, I'm not fine at all. What are we going to do, Jake?"

"I don't know," he replied. "But we better come up with something fast."

They hiked down the trail that ran alongside Lake Lola. Jake gazed out at the lake. A glittering, black shape broke the lake's surface and then disappeared. Probably an eel being chased by an arapaima, he thought. He had a brief—and slightly loony—vision of Cazador's sea serpent leaping out of the water to rescue them.

That's the problem with impossible animals, he thought. They're never around when you need them.

He tried to imagine what Professor Becker planned to do with them. Maybe he'll tie weights around their ankles and let them sink to the bottom of the lake. He immediately dismissed the idea. He didn't think they would do something so dramatic and messy. Becker probably didn't want Alaweed's employees witnessing a public execution.

Then, with a jolt of fear, he suddenly knew *exactly* where they were going and why their mother and the police would never find them.

"I just figured out where they're taking us," he said. "You're not going to like it."

"The Underzoo," she replied in a matter of fact way. "It's the only place that makes sense. Cazador told us that it wasn't far from the main compound." She glanced back at him, her face lined with worry. "Do you think we should make a run for it? Try to escape?"

Jake stared out at the barren landscape. Rocky hills framed the valley on both sides of them. "We could try, but there's no place to hide. Even if we managed to get away from the guards and make it into those rocks, they would just catch us."

They hiked for another mile down the narrow pathway that led south from the zoo. The trail rose and fell, hugging the hills to their right. At last, they descended into a small canyon that might once have been a quarry. There were large piles of rubble at the base of sheer cliff walls. Corroded railroad tracks and rusty mining cars lay abandoned around the site.

"Open it up!" shouted Becker.

A guard pressed an electronic device in his hand. One of the enormous piles of rubble shuddered and appeared to break in two. The piles parted slowly, revealing a massive steel door set into the mountainside. In a moment, the door slid open as well, revealing the gaping mouth of a cave.

The Underzoo.

The guards forced them toward the cave opening. Jake saw that the floor of the cave was strewn with trash and what appeared to be bones. He winced as a blast of putrid air hit him—the smell of dung, decay, and death. Pablo still clung to Miranda's shoulder, his golden fur reflecting the sunlight. His tiny snub nose wrinkled in disgust as he smelled the cave. The monkey gripped Miranda's arm tightly, making fearful squeaks.

Cazador gave them a reassuring smile, but he looked nervous. "Don't worry, *niños*," he said. "Markus will not get away with this."

"But he *is* getting away with it," replied Jake. "What are we going to do, doctor? Once we're in the Underzoo, will we ever get out again?"

Before the doctor could respond, Professor Becker strolled over to them. "Did you know that the Underzoo has always been my favorite part of the Z.I.A.?" he said. "You were so inconsiderate, shutting it down just before you took me on. I would have relished a guided tour."

Cazador glowered at the tall keeper. "I'd be happy to give you a tour right now," he growled, gripping his black staff so hard that his knuckles turned white.

Becker ignored him. "Do you know why I like the Under-zoo so much?" he continued. "Because the animals are out of sight, out of mind—which is where the three of you will be shortly."

"Think about what you're doing, Markus," Cazador pleaded. "You won. Do what you want with me. But these children are innocent. Let them go."

"But they're so curious!" exclaimed Becker. "I'm simply showing them the rest of your menagerie. I mean, as much money and time as you've spent on the Z.I.A., you spent even more on the Underzoo, didn't you? You fed your monsters, watered them, and made sure they were comfortable in their cells. I'm sure they'll be overjoyed to see the man who locked them away for all these years."

"You're insane, Markus," said the doctor. "Hiring you was the worst mistake I ever made in my life. In fact, professor—you're fired!"

For a moment, the pale keeper stared at the doctor in bewilderment. Then his face darkened. "Did you hear that everybody?" he shouted, glancing at the men behind him. "Cazador is firing me! That is hilarious, doctor. I'll miss your senile—"

But before he could finish his sentence, Cazador swung his staff at Becker's legs like a sword. The blow flipped the tall man onto his back where he landed with a hard thud. Instantly, the doctor was on top of him, gripping him roughly by the lapels of his shirt. Becker suddenly looked terrified.

"I'm giving you one more chance, Markus," Cazador yelled. "*Let these children go!*"

For a second, Jake thought Cazador would choke Becker to

death. Soon, however, Bolo rushed over, grabbing the doctor by his shoulders and throwing him off of the professor. Cazador landed next to Miranda and Jake in a cloud of dust. The professor scrambled to his feet and brushed the dirt from his khaki uniform. He picked up Cazador's black staff and hurled it angrily behind him.

"That wasn't very smart, doctor," Becker hissed, smoothing his blond hair back into place. "You're going to pay dearly for that little stunt."

He nodded at Bolo, who walked over to Cazador. From his belt, the hulking security man took out a steel rod the size of baton. With a flip of his wrist, he extended it until it was as long as a baseball bat. He took off his sunglasses and stared icily at the old doctor. Jake realized this was the first time he'd seen Bolo's eyes. It was like gazing into the eyes of a shark.

"Have a real nice tour of the Underzoo, doc," drawled Bolo, breaking into a malicious grin. "Sorry you're gonna have to spend most of the time on your hands and knees." In a flash, he brought the rod crashing down onto Cazador's right leg. It made a sickening crack. The doctor groaned and fell onto his side, his hands clutching his leg in agony. Miranda immediately knelt down beside him.

"You're such a coward, Bolo," yelled Jake. "Does Alaweed give you a raise every time you beat up a senior citizen?"

Bolo's eyes flashed with anger and Jake thought he'd be the next one on the ground. Instead, the tattooed man put his sunglasses back on and placed the rod back into his belt. "I did that one for free," he said. "Good luck down there, kid. You're gonna need it."

Jake and Miranda helped Cazador to his feet and together

they walked slowly into the cave. They heard a loud grinding noise as the steel doors began to shut behind them. They stared out at Becker, Feng, and Bolo as the long rectangle of sunlight illuminating the cave began to shrink. Finally, the door closed with a loud noise of metal on stone, followed by the sounds of gears turning.

Jake stared blankly into the pitch-black darkness. Somewhere in this cave, he thought, lived the most dangerous animals in the entire world.

He had a feeling they would be hungry.

23

Into the Underzoo

As they huddled together in the smelly darkness, Jake went over their options in his head. There were not many and they were all terrible.

Option one: Sit patiently and wait for Professor Becker to have pity on them and let them out. That wasn't going to happen. Option two: Dig their way out. In the dark. With their bare hands. That seemed even less likely and a lot more painful. Option three: Crawl around in the darkness until they found a passageway that would take them deeper into the cave.

And *then* what?

Oh, right, he thought. Then get eaten by a bunch of psychotic cryptids.

Bad, bad, and worse, he thought.

"Finally!" exclaimed Cazador. "I thought they'd *never* leave. Let's get to work."

It was Miranda who pointed out the obvious. "What are we supposed to do, doctor?" she asked. She sounded scared, even close to panic. "We're trapped in the Underzoo, you're injured, and we can't see anything in here."

"Injured? Ha!" Cazador's voice echoed around the cave. "That Bolo goon isn't half as strong as he thinks he is. And the situation isn't as hopeless as you think. We have several advantages that Markus failed to account for in his eagerness to get rid of us."

"What are you talking about?" said Jake. "We're stuck in your super-max prison for cryptids. The only advantage I see is that we won't get struck by lightning anytime soon. By the way, where are all the animals? Shouldn't we be running for our lives by now?"

"Believe me," replied Cazador. "If an Underzoo cryptid were in this chamber right now, we wouldn't be having this pleasant conversation. Assuming the cryptids are still alive at all, they'll be in the main chambers another mile into the mountain. Right now we're in the intake room where we used to load supplies. We need to be as far away from here as possible before Markus returns."

"What do you mean, doctor?" asked Miranda. "Why would he come back? I thought his goal was to leave us here to die."

"Oh, he'll be back," he said confidently. "He'll be back because he needs *this!*" Light suddenly bloomed in the darkness, revealing Cazador's grinning face. In his hand, he held a black device not much bigger than a cell phone. Its screen gave off a brilliant white light.

"The crypticon!" Jake shouted.

"How did you get it?" asked Miranda. "Professor Becker had it at the tower. I saw him put it in his jacket."

The doctor scratched his beard and smiled sheepishly. "Remember my scuffle with Markus outside the cave? I wasn't *really* trying to strangle him, even though he is a traitorous rat. Well, maybe I was trying to strangle him a little. Mostly, I was picking his pocket."

"You stole the crypticon from Becker while you were on

the ground?" asked Jake, dumbfounded. "That is so awesome!"

"I had no choice. This is one of only two crypticons in the entire world. The other is with Dembi and Cormick in Africa. I can't have it falling into the hands of Alaweed. When Markus discovers the crypticon is missing, he'll know I took it and he'll send Bolo after us. We don't want to be here when that happens."

Cazador handed Miranda the crypticon and they helped him to his feet. The doctor put his hand on their shoulders and they shuffled toward the back of the cave. Miranda pointed the crypticon in front of them so they could see where they were going. They stopped in front of a heavy steel door. Cazador slid open a panel on the wall next to it and entered a code on an electronic pad. They heard a beeping sound as small lights appeared on the pad. The door began to open.

"This door separates the intake chamber from the tunnel that leads to the heart of the Underzoo," he explained. "It allowed my keepers to load the rail car with food without fear of the cryptids escaping—or eating them." He glanced at the crypticon and then peered into the darkness. "It looks clear. No welcome party at the moment."

As another blast of foul-smelling air hit them, they saw an arched tunnel near the back wall. In front of it, there was a mini-train with four seats and a flatbed in back. It sat on steel rails that led into the tunnel.

"Thank goodness the entry pad worked," said Cazador, limping into the chamber. "That means the power is still on. Do you have the Bestiary? I placed it in Tuan's locker before I was captured. He *did* give it to you, didn't he?"

"So *you* were the one who left it?" asked Miranda. "It's in my backpack. Why did you leave it for us?"

"I didn't want Markus and Alaweed to get their hands on it," he replied. "It's the only copy. Also, in light of our present situation, we're going to need it."

"Why?" asked Jake. "Don't you know all the cryptids in the Underzoo?"

"Yes, of course," said Cazador. "But it's been years since I've been down here. I don't remember where I put them all. The bestiary has a map."

They followed him over to the metal car on the tracks. "So you used to take this thing into the Underzoo?" asked Miranda, still holding the crypticon in front of her like a flashlight.

"That's correct," he said, easing himself gingerly into the front seat of the machine. "It's a maglev mini-train. It uses magnets to create both lift and propulsion to move down the track. Later, we used it as a remote controlled vehicle to deliver the cryptids food once a month. I halted all shipments years ago."

"So if we're riding on it won't the cryptids think *we're* food?" asked Jake.

He frowned. "I hadn't thought of that," remarked Cazador. "I suppose they might. However, unless you want to take a long walk in the dark, we don't have another choice. As dangerous as the beasts of the Underzoo are, they're not our immediate concern."

As if on cue, they heard a grinding noise near the cave entrance. "It's the boulder wall opening outside!" Miranda exclaimed. "They're coming back."

"As I predicted," said the doctor. "We must leave now."

They sat down behind him in the car. Miranda gently took

Pablo from her shoulder and placed him on her lap. The monkey looked surprisingly calm given the circumstances. Its oval eyes peered curiously around the cave.

"More light, please," said Cazador. "I need to switch the controls to manual."

Miranda held up the crypticon as the doctor fiddled with the console, which was located where a steering wheel should have been. Jake looked around for seat belts. No luck. In the room behind them, a shaft of sunlight pierced the darkness as the steel door began to open. Black-uniformed men with rifles began pouring into the cave.

"Find 'em!" someone shouted. It was Bolo. "Shoot 'em if you have to, but don't hit the crypticon or I'll leave you here to rot!"

"Anytime now, doctor," said Jake anxiously. "We're about to have lots of company and they don't sound happy."

"Hurry, hurry, hurry," urged Miranda. "They're almost here!"

Suddenly, a dozen colored lights appeared on the console and the cart started to hum. "*Perfecto!*" Cazador exclaimed, pressing one of the blinking red buttons. "Hold onto the bar in front of you. The maglev is smooth as ice, but it's quite fast. Please try not to throw up."

With a jolt, the car began to move down the tracks. They heard a shout from the direction of the men as Bolo and his crew saw them. Pablo wrapped his tail around Miranda's arm, burying his tiny, blue face against her. The car sped up as they entered the tunnel.

Cazador grinned and gave them a thumbs-up sign. "Keep your hands and feet in the vehicle at all times. This will make every roller coaster you've ever been on feel like a leisurely drive to the grocery store."

Cazador was actually *enjoying* himself! thought Jake. He didn't know if this made him feel better or worse about their chances. As they plunged into the darkness, he found one Miranda's hands and held onto it tightly.

Within a few seconds, it felt like they didn't have enough breath in their lungs even to scream.

24

A One-Way Ticket Down

The tunnel swallowed up all light and noise, casting them into a world of wind, speed, and darkness. To Jake, it felt as if he were on a rocket ship blasting into space. His stomach jumped into his throat as the car pitched downward into nothingness. A few seconds later, he slammed against his seat as it zoomed upward. Then the process repeated itself a dozen nauseating times. What made the ride even weirder was that the maglev never made a noise. It glided soundlessly down the tracks without a bump or vibration.

After what felt like an eternity, the train slowed. The wind in Jake's face now seemed less forceful and his stomach calmed down. He wiped the tears that had involuntarily leaked out of the corners of his eyes.

"Um, Jake?" shouted Miranda above the noise of wind. "You're crushing my hand."

"Oh, sorry." He switched his grip to the bar in front of him. He couldn't see her in the pitch blackness, even though he knew she sat only inches away. "How are you doing? This is pretty crazy, huh?"

"It would actually be fun if I weren't so freaked out," she said. "At least we got away from Bolo and his gang. I wish we could ride this maglev back to our house."

"Me, too. The worst thing about this ride is that when it stops we might get gobbled up."

"Grow up, Jake," she said. "That's not funny."

He grunted. "For once, I wasn't trying to be funny."

Cazador turned his head back to face them. "We should be entering the ballroom any moment now."

The ballroom? thought Jake. Are they going to be fighting the cryptids or dancing with them?

The sound of the wind ceased and the air grew warmer, almost humid. Jake suddenly had the feeling of being inside a very large space. "How long do we have until something tries to eat us, doctor?" he asked.

"I'm still not convinced that anything will eat us," he replied. "If we're lucky, the cryptids will have eaten each other by now. In any case, we should be safe this far above the cave floor for a while." He turned back toward the front. "I'm going to stop the maglev. Hold on."

Blue and red lights reappeared on the dashboard. After a series of beeps, the train came to a sudden stop, jerking them forward in their seats. Cazador turned on the crypticon. Its light revealed a steep stone wall and a narrow cement pathway to their right. "Get out on the right side of the train or your first step will be your last. Follow the lights along the path."

Before they could ask him which lights he was talking about, a tiny fluorescent bulb next to the maglev flickered to life. It was immediately joined by dozens of others at regular intervals along the tracks that led down to the floor of the cavern a hundred yards away. Soon there were thousands of lights in the cave—on walls, floors, even along the ceiling.

Jake and Miranda stared in amazement as the cavern

154

slowly grew visible in the pale glow. The maglev seemed to be perched on a narrow ridge carved into one side of the cavern. On the other side was a sheer drop of two hundred feet. They could make out the outlines of the cave, including several arched tunnel entrances in the distant walls below them. To their relief, there were no signs of life below.

Not yet anyway, thought Jake.

They unbuckled their seatbelts and cautiously stepped onto the narrow ledge next to the tracks.

"My beautiful ballroom!" exclaimed Cazador, looking mournfully around the huge cave. "What have they done to you?"

As the doctor limped down the trail, Miranda tugged Jake's arm. "I think I saw something down there. See? There are shapes moving among the boulders."

Jake peered at the cave floor. "I don't see anything. Maybe it's just shadows from all those lights. Come on. Let's catch up to Cazador."

The trail widened slightly as they hiked down the tracks. Soon, they arrived at a recessed area carved into the rock wall. Small lights glowed at the base of a metal door.

Cazador glanced down at the crypticon. "I don't think anything is in the ballroom yet," he said. "We're safe for now."

"So the crypticon tells you exactly which cryptids are here?" asked Miranda.

"As long as they're within a hundred meters of us," he said. "I'm going to send the maglev to the end of the tracks. If anything is in the ballroom outside the range of the crypticon, this should bring them out of their hidey holes."

The rail car zipped past them with a barely audible hum.

"Why do you call this place the ballroom?" Jake asked, as they watched the maglev glide down the track. "Kind of a weird name for a creepy cave."

"My keepers nicknamed some of the Underzoo's chambers," replied Cazador. "Since this is one of the largest caverns, they called it the ballroom. This place was magnificent! It had viewing stands, offices, a cafeteria, even a basketball court. Of course, this was before the cryptids went *loco* and destroyed it all."

Miranda still gaze nervously at the cave floor. "So what's your plan, doctor? I mean, you *do* have a plan, don't you?"

"A plan!" He tugged at his beard, deep in thought. "Yes, we need a plan." Jake looked at Miranda and they exchanged worried glances. "I think our best hope is the emergency entrance at the north end of the cave. The tricky part will be getting there without running into any surviving cryptids or Bolo and his men, unless they gave up already."

Suddenly, they heard a series of loud beeps from the crypticon. Cazador looked down at the device. Yellow lights filled the screen. He cursed in Spanish. "So much for our being alone down here." he said. "It makes sense that these would be the first ones to greet us. Greedy *maldiciones!*"

Jake and Miranda looked down at the cave floor. Ominous shapes oozed out of the darkness. At first, they appeared to be dogs. But instead of fur, their bodies were covered in black scabs or scales. Thin, needle-like spikes protruded along their spines. The creatures moved cautiously toward the maglev until they completely surrounded it.

The sight of the cryptids sent a chill through Jake's body. "What *are* those things?" he asked.

"Chupacabras," said Cazador, his voice dripping with disgust. "We found a den of them in Puerto Rico fifteen years ago. They're obviously thriving here. They're like hairless, scabby hyenas, but far more vicious. They can survive as scavengers, but they prefer their prey alive. That way they can suck the blood from them."

"Suck their blood?" exclaimed Miranda, horrified. "What are they? Vampires?"

"If Dracula had a pet, I believe it would be a chupacabra," he replied matter of factly. "A single chupacabra by itself is alarming, but hardly life-threatening. However, a pack of them can terrorize a village for weeks."

Suddenly, the chupacabras began to howl. It was a piercing, high-pitched noise that echoed through the cave. After about a minute, the howling stopped and the animals melted back into the shadows of the cave as mysteriously as they had arrived.

"What happened?" asked Jake, his ears ringing. "Why did they leave?"

Cazador studied the crypticon. "I don't know. Something must have scared them away."

"What could frighten away a pack of vampire dogs?" asked Miranda.

A sharp pinging noise came from the crypticon as lights filled the screen. Cazador's face grew pale. "Amaroks," he said in a whisper. "I don't see them yet, but they're here. We must get inside *now!*"

25

A Desperate Plan

Cazador limped over to the panel and punched in the code. They heard a soft click as the door opened. Fluorescent lights on the room's ceiling flickered on as they entered.

It seemed to be a work room, thought Jake. There were white cabinets, a sink, several chairs, and a table. There was even an old copy machine. Everything was covered in a thick layer of black dust. He glanced at Miranda, who looked pale and exhausted. Her uniform was torn at the right knee and her name tag hung from her shirt by a few threads. Her long brown hair was tangled and stringy. She was still carrying Pablo, who seemed more agitated. Probably hungry, he thought. Or maybe he smelled the other cryptids.

"You're a mess, Jake," said Miranda, gently placing Pablo on the table. The monkey began exploring the room. "I mean, more than usual."

"Funny," he said, grinning. "I was just thinking the same thing about you. At least you still have your lousy sense of humor." He looked over at Cazador. "Where are we right now, doctor? This place feels like a teacher's lounge."

"I suppose it is in a way," replied the doctor. "This is a break room for the keepers. There were several similar rooms throughout the Underzoo, but this is the only one that is still intact. This will be our safe house until the amaroks are gone. In the meantime, I need to figure out how to get us to that back service entrance."

He hobbled over to the table and eased himself into one of the chairs. "I need to review the bestiary's map. Why don't you two rummage through the cabinets? Keep anything that looks useful."

While Cazador paged through the bestiary, Jake and Miranda went over to the white cabinets lining the wall. "Did you see how nasty those chupacabras looked?" Jake whispered. "They were right out of a horror movie. Can you imagine getting cornered by a pack of those guys?"

"No, I can't," said Miranda, opening one of the cabinets. It was crammed with paper, printer cartridges, and other office supplies. "But we just got here. Maybe we'll get to find out." She opened another cabinet and her eyes lit up. "Water!" She pulled a large plastic carton from the cabinet. "And a canteen."

Cazador glanced up from the book. "Good work! Keep searching."

The other cabinets were useless. There were staplers, paper towels, ink pens (which Pablo confiscated immediately), coffee filters, napkins, and utensils.

"None of this is going to help us," mumbled Jake. "Unless we want to throw an office party."

In the last cabinet, they found a black container that looked like a heavy-duty duffel bag. Jake pulled it out and put it on the table. "What is this, Cazador?" he asked.

Cazador examined the case. "Well done. This is quite a stroke of luck."

"Why? What's in it?" asked Miranda as they sat down at the table.

The doctor pulled the bag toward him and unkipped it. "This is a cryptid kit. We prepare specialized kits for different missions. This is the one for the Underzoo. We must have forgotten to take it with us when we abandoned the zoo."

He began removing items from the bag, examining each of them one by one before placing it on the table. "Everything is here—first-aid kit, LED flashlight, multi-tool, rope, hunting knife, flare gun, pepper spray, compass. And this!" He held up a thin chrome object.

"What is *that?*" asked Jake. "Some kind of futuristic fishing pole?"

"You *could* try fishing with it, but I would advise against it," replied Cazador. "This is a high-powered tranquilizer rifle. Polymer frame, three-inch barrel, twenty ounces, 13-round magazine. It uses fifty-caliber bullets and gas canisters. Each dart has an explosive charge that detonates on impact and quickly injects the drug." He held up one of the hypodermic darts. "Each dart is filled with M-99—Etorphine hydrochloride. Dangerous stuff. It won't stop an emela-ntouka, but it will knock out most of the creatures down here."

Jake whistled appreciatively. "That's the coolest thing I've ever seen in my life."

Miranda frowned. "What about the map, doctor? Did you find a way to the back entrance?"

Cazador put the gun down on the table. "Yes, I did," he said. "Help me spread the map out on the table."

The map of the Underzoo didn't resemble any map Jake had ever seen. It resembled a long snake with its stomach bellied-out in different places, as if it had eaten a dozen elephants. It had labels identifying various chambers and the corridors that linked them together.

"This shows the cave system that makes up the old Sierra Vista silver mine," Cazador explained. "The mining company abandoned it back in the 1950s. When I bought it, it was still in relatively good shape. Of course, we vastly improved and expanded it." He pointed to an area inside the first of the cave's large chambers. "We're right here." He dragged his finger across the map through six of the chambers in the snake's body to another large circle on the right edge of the map. "To reach the old service entrance, we have to make it over here. It's a couple miles of corridors."

"It seems really far away," said Miranda worriedly. "How will we be able to get there with amaroks and chupacabras roaming around?"

Cazador tugged at his beard nervously. "It won't be easy," he replied. "And given the fact that the larger mammals such as the chupacabras and amaroks are still alive, I have to assume that other cryptids are as well. There are some truly unpleasant characters in the Underzoo. At least this map gives us a chance to avoid them. We just have to hope there haven't been any cave-ins in the corridors."

"Cave-ins?" asked Jake. This day kept getting better and better, he thought miserably. "You mean, like rocks-falling-on-our heads-burying-us-alive cave-ins?"

Cazador nodded. "In spite of our geo-engineering, sections of the cave collapse now and then. The Underzoo is still a part of nature."

"How large *is* the Underzoo?" asked Miranda.

"It's vast. When I found it, the mine had dozens of chambers. We sealed off smaller passages and consolidated larger ones until we had ten or so immense rooms."

"So the bulges are the enclosures?" she asked. "And all these lines are the corridors that connect them?"

"Precisely," he said. "When I brought the animals down here, I placed them in various enclosures located within each of these ten sections. It worked well for a while, but we soon discovered that there were hidden passages we never found, let alone sealed. By the end of the first year, some cryptids were roaming wherever they wanted."

He pointed at the bubble representing the third chamber. "For example, amaroks are supposed to be confined to this chamber here. Obviously, that's not the case anymore. However, I'm hoping we can avoid these larger cryptids by using this narrow corridor here." He tapped a blue oval in the seventh chamber. "It's the only one that doesn't feed into Lost Lake."

"Why don't we just use one of the corridors that goes directly to Lost Lake?" asked Jake. "Any of them would get us out of here faster."

The doctor shook his head. "We must avoid Lost Lake at all costs. It's the only source of water in the cave, so it will be a gathering place for cryptids. No, we'll stick to the passageway on the other side of the tenth chamber. That corridor should put us out near the old service entrance."

"But won't the professor send men to guard that entrance?" asked Miranda.

"It's possible," admitted Cazador. "But Markus doesn't know the Underzoo's exact layout. Besides, he's probably too busy fending off the police and coordinating the sale of my animals."

"So you think all the cryptids down here are still alive?" asked Jake.

The doctor scratched his beard. "Ten years ago we placed two dozen different cryptids in the Underzoo. What we saw in the ballroom tells me that not only are most of them still alive, they're thriving." He placed the crypticon on the table and tapped the screen. "The good news is that with the crypticon we can identify all cryptids within 100 meters. The lighted dots correspond to specific bio signatures. Each animal has its own color. We're the white dot in the center of the screen. As we've seen the yellow dots represent chupacabras. Red dots are amaroks."

A series of furious beeps suddenly erupted from the device. Jake pointed at the screen. "So what are those red dots doing way up here by the white dot?" he asked. "Doesn't that mean—"

They heard a loud banging on the metal entry door to the room. Something large sniffed furiously at the narrow gap beneath the door. Suddenly, deafening howls filled the room as the door bowed inwardly for a moment against the weight of something very strong. The howls sounded deeper and louder than those of the chupacabras.

Nobody needed the crypticon to tell them that the amaroks had arrived.

26

Amaroks at the Door

They stared at the door, paralyzed by fear. Cazador was the first to speak. "Go to that monitor on the wall and press the black button. Hurry. As quietly as you can."

Miranda and Jake got up from the table and went over to a small rectangular box on the wall. Miranda pressed one of the buttons and the screen flickered to life. "There's a security camera outside the door," continued Cazador. "I probably should have remembered that earlier."

After a few seconds, the screen of the black wall-mounted device flickered on. It was an image of a large, yellow eyeball.

"Is that what I think it is?" asked Jake.

Cazador stood slowly to his feet. "That is an amarok. It seems to be very interested in the camera above the door."

When Pablo glimpsed the image of the eyeball, he scurried over to Miranda and leaped into her arms. "It's OK, boy," she whispered. "We're in here. He's out there."

"For *now*," said Jake. "Look at the size of him. How many of them are out there?"

The eyeball suddenly disappeared and they were able to see what was going on. There were three amaroks outside the door. They growled and occasionally nipped at each other, banging against the door as if testing its strength. The animals resembled wolves, but they were almost as large as horses. The biggest one had completely black fur with bright, yellow eyes. The fur seemed thickest around its powerful head and shoulders, almost like a lion's mane. Its paws looked as big and heavy as frying pans.

"Those things are huge," said Miranda in awe. "And look at their teeth!"

Each of the amaroks had two long teeth as thick as steak knives that jutted upwards from their lower jaws. It was the opposite of where a normal wolf's canines would be, thought Jake. It gave the animals an angry, almost psychotic look.

All of a sudden, one of the amaroks lunged at the camera. There was a crashing noise outside the door that made Jake and Miranda stumble backwards toward the table. For a moment, the screen revealed the flashing white teeth of the amarok as it furiously attacked the camera. Then the screen went black. They looked at the device on the wall for a few seconds, too shocked to speak. The howling started again.

"The amarok ate the camera," said Jake, stunned. "It's as if it knew we were watching."

Cazador handed Jake the tranquilizer gun. "Be careful— that's loaded. Put as many of the cryptid kit items into the backpack as you can. Jake, you take the gun and the pack. Miranda, get Pablo and the water."

A thunderous sound like a giant drum echoed around the room as an amarok crashed into the door again. Dust from the ceiling tiles floated to the floor. Miranda looked worriedly over at Cazador. "How strong is that door, doctor?" she asked.

"Not strong enough," he said grimly. "A few more assaults and the amaroks will knock it down like that wolf that blew down the houses of those little pigs."

"Didn't one of the pigs build a house that the wolf couldn't destroy?" asked Jake.

Cazador sighed. "Let's just say I haven't been the smartest pig where the Underzoo is concerned. Now let's get ready."

They positioned themselves on either side of the door. The howls and barks intensified and a horrible odor filled the room—the scent of a wet dog that had lived in a sewer for a year. Jake's hands were shaking as he held the rifle. He had serious doubts that the gun would work on even one amarok, let alone three. Beneath the door, a glistening pool of saliva oozed across the tile. Then there was a single, mournful howl, as if from far away. The animals by the door answered the howl with a bone-chilling chorus of their own. There was a furious commotion outside the door and then silence. After a minute, Pablo snatched one of the pens from Miranda's pocket and began to chew on it contentedly.

"Pablo, at least, thinks the danger has passed," remarked Cazador.

"What happened?" asked Jake. "Did they just leave?"

Miranda walked up to the door and put her ear against it. "They found easier prey," she said. "That's the only explanation. Bolo and his crew must be heading down the maglev tunnel. I bet the amaroks went to check them out."

"I think you might be right," said Cazador. "That's good and bad news. I was hoping that Bolo would have given up, but now we have a chance to get across the ballroom to those corridors on the other side."

Jake put on the backpack. "You stay with Cazador," he told Miranda. "Open the door just enough to let me slide through.

166

I'll let you know if it's safe to come out."

"That's sweet of you, Jake," she said, patting his shoulder. "No offense, but you couldn't even handle a few stinky lizards by yourself. We're going with you."

Cazador smiled. "You two make a formidable team. I almost feel sorry for the cryptids."

Jake turned the bolt on the door and slowly pushed it open. They stared into the ghostly light of the cave for a moment before stepping through the door. Jake held the gun in front of him as they walked toward the maglev tracks. There was a distant, solitary howl from the tunnel above them, followed by faint popping noises.

"Gun shots," said Cazador. "You were right, Miranda. Bolo and his men are getting to know the guard dogs of the Underzoo." He pointed across the ballroom. "Can you see the entrances against the far wall?" Beyond the maglev, there were three arched openings in the wall. They were partially obscured by piles of rock and several big boulders. "The tunnel on the far right leads to the service corridor. That's our destination. I'll take the lead. Point the flashlight on the ground in front of me, *señorita*. I don't want to fall off the cliff. Jake, you bring up the rear."

They began the hike down the slope toward the cavern floor. For Jake, it felt like walking from the top seats of a sports stadium to the field. The only difference was that once they got down there, the players might eat them.

The cave floor was flat and paved almost entirely with bricks. The buildings might have been nice a long time ago, but now they were crumbling and spooky. Animal bones and clumps of brown stuff that must have been cryptid poop were scattered everywhere.

"Gross," muttered Miranda. "Watch your step, Jake. This place is more disgusting than your bedroom."

"But it's a lot nicer than your bathroom," he quipped.

They stopped next to the maglev and peered into the gloom. Cazador pointed ahead of them to the far side of the chamber. "We're not alone," he said. "Look over there."

At first, they could see only the far rock wall jutting toward the cave ceiling and a few towering boulders. Then they saw a row of dark shapes standing directly across their path like a low hedge.

A hedge with yellow eyes, thought Jake.

"Chupacabras," Cazador whispered. "Don't move. Turn off the flashlight."

Miranda clicked off the light. The gloom in the ballroom became thicker and more oppressive. The line of chupacabras was clearly visible now. "They're a lot smaller than amaroks," remarked Jake. "Maybe we can throw some rocks at them and scare them away."

Cazador shook his head. "It will take more than rocks to frighten away a chupacabra," he said. "We must be very careful here."

One of the chupacabras abruptly broke away from the line and slouched toward them. As it passed through a circle of light, they saw what they were dealing with. The creature was about the size of a German shepherd, but all similarities to a dog ended there. It was hairless and scabby, with sharp spines poking out of its back. It stopped ten feet away from them and sniffed the air, moving its head back and forth like a cobra. Razor-sharp teeth glistened wetly as it curled back its lips into a snarl. It stared at them with black, lifeless eyes.

"It looks like a zombie coyote," whispered Miranda. "What's it doing, Cazador?"

"It's trying to figure out how much of a fight we'll put up," he said quietly. "We're running out of time. It will be a disaster if we're trapped here between Bolo and the chupacabras."

"Are they afraid of fire?" asked Jake. "Maybe we could use the flares."

"Brilliant, *mi hijo!*" exclaimed the doctor. "Miranda, get the flare gun from your brother's backpack. There should be a packet of flares as well. Hurry!"

Jake turned and knelt down so that Miranda could rummage through the pack. "Found it!" she said, handing the gun and flares to Cazador.

The doctor took a flare and fastened it onto the end of the gun like a cork in a bottle. "These flares are 200 times brighter than a light bulb," he said. "They also sound like the loudest firecracker you've ever heard. After I shoot the third one, I want you to run toward the tunnel entrance. If a chupacabra attacks you, Jake, use the rifle. I'll be right behind you."

As he spoke, the chupacabra began to edge closer. Its two, needle-like canines were now clearly visible. Fangs, thought Jake. These things really *were* vampire dogs.

"Are you ready?" asked Cazador. They nodded. He pointed the flare gun above the pack of animals and pulled the trigger.

The noise was like a clap of thunder. A red arc soared over the heads of the massed chupacabras, ricocheted against the wall, and bounced back into the pack. He fired off two more flares in quick succession.

"Run!" shouted Cazador. "I'll meet you in the tunnel!"

Jake and Miranda sprinted across the ballroom, scrambling over rocks, bones, and other debris. In the bright light of the flare, they could see chupacabras scattering in every direction. Jake held the tranquilizer rifle in his left hand, but the animals took no interest in them. In fact, one almost ran into them in its frantic attempt to escape. The entrance was now only twenty feet away. Suddenly, a chupacabra halted directly in front of them, sniffing the air, its body bathed in the flare's red glow. It swiveled its grotesque head toward them and snarled, exposing a row of teeth as sharp as scalpels.

Jake brought up the tranquilizer rifle, took aim, and squeezed the trigger. With a low thumping sound, the gun jumped in his hands as it expelled the dart, which embedded itself into the animal's side. The chupacabra stumbled, staring at them as if surprised, and then promptly fell over onto its side.

"Nice shot!" Miranda shouted, grabbing his hand. "Now let's go!"

Less than a minute later they collapsed onto the ground just inside the entrance. Breathless and shaking, they turned around to see what was happening in the ballroom.

The flares had worked. The chupacabras seemed to have fled the scene. Only then did they realize that the doctor wasn't with them.

"Where did Cazador go?" asked Jake. "I thought he was right behind us."

"I don't know," replied Miranda, looking around. "Do you think he fell down?"

"Wait—I think I see him," Jake peered into the ballroom. "Over there by the maglev."

In the red light of the dying flares, they saw Cazador swinging wildly at two chupacabras with what appeared to be a sword. Then the flares went out and everything was plunged into gloomy semi-darkness again. As Jake's eyes adjusted again to the dim light, something drew his attention to the ballroom entrance.

Five twinkling lights—much brighter than the pale fluorescent lights of the cave—emerged near the area where the maglev tracks entered the cave. After a pause, the lights continued slowly down the tracks.

Jake and Miranda looked at each other. Bolo and his men had made it past the amaroks.

27

Attack of the Mahambas

anic gripped Jake as he watched the men with flashlights follow the maglev tracks down the hill. If Bolo and his mercenaries were able to fight off a pack of vicious wolves the size of bulls, he thought, what chance did *they* have?

"Bolo's coming," said Miranda. "What are we going to do now?"

"I don't know," replied Jake. "I wish that guy would find a new hobby or something. He's got to have something better to do than chase us around."

Someone stumbled out from behind a nearby boulder. He hobbled over to them, his face pale and wild. It was Cazador.

They ran over to him. "Are you all right?" asked Miranda. "We saw you fighting with some chupacabras. What are you holding?"

He glanced down at the rusty weapon in his hand as if he were surprised to see it. "A machete. I found it by the maglev." He looked at Jake. "Where's your rifle?"

Jake felt for the gun, which had been hanging on his shoulder. "Oh, man," he said apologetically. "The strap must have broken."

Cazador frowned. "That's too bad because—"

He was cut off by the loud crack of a gunshot. They winced as the bullet ricocheted off the cave ceiling.

"That was a warning shot, Cazador," shouted Bolo, his deep, rumbling drawl echoing across the cave. "Cool your jets a minute. We need to talk."

Bolo and his men had made it all the way down the maglev tracks and were now only a hundred feet away. One of his men was limping, his right leg wrapped in a blood-soaked cloth.

"I'm assuming Markus sent you back for this?" yelled Cazador, holding up the crypticon. "Alaweed must pay you very well indeed for you to venture into the Underzoo."

"As a matter of fact, they doubled my already outrageous fee," replied Bolo, flashing his jackal grin. "What they don't know is that I plan to double it again before I hand 'em that little gadget of yours." The smile disappeared. "Now can we discuss this situation like reasonable people? Or do you want to wait around until those devil dogs catch up to us?"

"Talk all you want," replied the doctor. "But if you take one step closer, I'll destroy the crypticon. Knowing Alaweed, if you come back without it, the Underzoo will be your new home."

Bolo looked calm, almost relaxed. "Look, Doc, it wasn't my idea to throw you down here," he shouted. "No siree! I told the professor: 'Lock 'em up in the tower. Keep 'em out of the way till we're gone.' But that Becker—he's a cranky one. And the prince hates your guts, too. I just do what they tell me to do."

As Bolo spoke, the crypticon began to beep softly. Cazador glanced down at it. His eyebrows shot up in surprise. He tilted the device so that Jake and Miranda could see the screen. "Do you notice anything different?" he whispered.

There were dozens of colored lights on the screen. Jake

knew that meant there were a lot of cryptids within a hundred meters of them. Most of them were clustered on the edge of the screen, but six purple dots were moving in a line directly toward them. Fast.

"Those purple ones," whispered Miranda. "What are they?"

"Those are mahambas," he said. "Get ready to run."

Cazador looked back at Bolo, who was still talking. "I think we'll keep the crypticon for now, Mr. Young," he said, cutting him off. "I hope you have a lovely time in the Underzoo. Next time, I advise you against blindly following orders, even if you're being paid a lot of money." He paused. "You might also want to find a better place to hide."

Bolo frowned. "What are talking about, you crazy old—" His words were cut short by a strange noise coming from one end of the ballroom. It sounded like concrete blocks being dragged across the floor. The ground began to vibrate.

"Quick! Into the tunnel!" Cazador told Miranda and Jake. "There's no time to lose!"

As they ran into the tunnel, a herd of enormous animals exploded out of the darkness. Each one was as long as a speed boat, with jaws like crocodiles and overlapping teeth as big as ice-cream cones. Their hides were as white as milk, with streaks of black along their sides and back. They thrashed their tails behind them, propelling themselves toward Bolo and his men, who began to sprint up the maglev tracks toward the ballroom entrance. The mahamba in front snapped its jaws as the pack rumbled past the tunnel entrance in which Cazador, Jake and Miranda stood. One of the mahambas near the back of the pack slowed down in front of the tunnel. It turned its massive head until it was looking directly at them, its coal-black eyes narrowing.

"Look at that one," shouted Miranda, pointing at one of the animals. "What is it doing?"

"Do you really want to wait and find out? said Jake. "Let's get out of here!"

"*Ándale!*" screamed Cazador. "Go, go, *GO!*"

With the flashlight in front of her, Miranda sprinted down the dark corridor. They could hear the sounds of gunfire behind them. There were no fluorescent lights in the tunnel, but the floor was free of rubble. After two hundred feet, the passage separated into two.

"Aim the light this way, Miranda," urged Cazador, gesturing to the right-hand corridor.

They stared at the area revealed in the flashlight's beam. An immense pile of rocks had completely blocked the right corridor. "*Qué horror!*" exclaimed the doctor. "It's just as I feared."

"What should we do?" asked Miranda. "Do we have to go back?"

"Did you see the size of those things?" asked Jake, trying to catch his breath. "There's no *way* we're going back there! Let's just take this other corridor. It looks safe enough to me."

"It is most certainly *not* safe," replied Cazador sternly. "But now we have no choice."

"Why? Where does it lead?" asked Miranda.

"It takes us directly through the enclosures. Undoubtedly, many of the cryptids that once lived in those areas will still be there. Except after all this commotion, they'll be ready."

"Ready for what?" asked Jake.

"Ready for *us*," he replied.

23

Forest of the Dead

A s they made their way down the corridor, Cazador's pace slowed. He became cautious, halting frequently to listen for signs of pursuit or to consult the map. Jake looked at Miranda, who still had Pablo on her shoulder. She seemed to be in good spirits, considering everything they'd been through.

He wondered what their mother was doing. If she had gotten home from work, it would not take her long to start to worry about them. By six, she would contact the police. Eventually, they would go to the Z.I.A. and interview Professor Becker, who would spin a tale about how the zoo's new tyros were on a plane to Africa.

He seriously doubted their mother would believe Becker's lies—even with a forged note from Miranda. Even at their most irresponsible, they'd never fly half way around the world without her permission. But even if she didn't believe the professor, what could the police do? They would take names, file a report, and try to contact the keepers in Africa. Then they'd check back in a day or two. That would give Becker and Alaweed all the time they needed to steal the rest of the cryptids and leave the country. It was a depressing thought.

Cazador held up his hand for them to stop. "We're almost

to the first enclosure. We need to be very careful here. The crypticon doesn't indicate anything, but it's not always accurate. Stay alert."

Not always accurate? thought Jake. *Now* he tells us.

The air felt warmer and more humid compared to the ballroom. It also didn't smell of dung and rotten meat any more. In fact, there was a faint but pleasant aroma of flowers.

"It smells like the National Botanic Garden in D.C.," said Miranda. "I used to go there with Mom all the time. There must be flowers nearby."

"I don't think so," Cazador said darkly. "Not in the Underzoo. We reserved this area for the *umdhlebi*—a deadly flowering plant from central Africa. But they should all be dead by now. I don't understand."

The corridor emptied into a cavernous chamber much smaller than the ballroom. As in the other enclosures, tiny lights lined the cave ceiling. In front of them, like guards standing at attention, were dozens of strange trees. Cazador clicked off the flashlight as they went down the paved walkway that appeared to cut across the jungly enclosure. Inside the chamber, the warm, rose-scented air was nearly overpowering.

Miranda stared at the tree-like plants in awe. "They're so peaceful and beautiful. Why did you put these down here? These don't look harmful at all."

"Don't forget the four laws, Miranda," said the doctor patiently. "Appearances are almost always deceiving when it comes to cryptids. Trust me—the umdhlebi is a killer."

They walked past the first tree, which stood to the right of the path. Its huge green leaves hung down like elephant ears. Its trunk was covered with curling pieces of black bark like peeled skin. Beneath its bark, they could see a fresh layer that glistened redly like an open wound. At the tree's base there was a thick carpet of roots and soil with white sticks jutting out in crazy angles. Underneath the floral perfume smell, Jake began to notice the foul odor of rotting meat. He examined the white things half-hidden in the soil.

"Oh, gross!" he exclaimed. "Are those animal bones beneath the trees?"

Cazador sat down on a bench overlooking the chamber. "They're the decaying bodies of chupacabras to be exact. I think I spotted the remains of a hatchling yacumama as well. You'll find decomposing animals beneath every tree."

"A yacumama?" asked Miranda. "I think I saw that one in the bestiary. It's some kind of giant snake, right?"

Cazador nodded as he stared out at the silent grove. "If yacumamas have survived down here, that's one more reason we must avoid Lost Lake, since they live primarily in water."

"I still don't understand why the umdhlebi trees are in the Underzoo," began Miranda. "I mean, they're disgusting and everything, but they don't exactly have claws and teeth. They can't move. They're harmless."

He shook his head. "Unfortunately, that's not true. We had a grove of them once at the Z.I.A. I couldn't figure out why my keepers who were tending them kept growing ill. Finally, one of the men died. After that, I incinerated most of the trees and placed the remaining ones down here. I thought they might be a food source for the animals."

"You had it backwards, doctor," said Miranda. "The animals became a food source for the umdhlebi."

"That's fascinating and everything," interrupted Jake impatiently. "But don't we have bigger issues right now? Like—I don't know—escaping from the Underzoo? How do we get through this chamber without getting sick or dying?"

"I'm not exactly sure," Cazador replied. He tugged at his silver beard, thinking. "What we know about umdhlebi plants comes from a notoriously unreliable paper from 1882 by Reverend Elihu Parker. Parker believed the plant emitted a lethal gas from its roots. But he could never prove—"

"Got it—poison plants," said Jake, interrupting him. "If we stay on the path and don't get too close to the roots, we'll be able to make it through the grove. Easy peasy."

The doctor stood up and stretched his back. "In theory, yes," he replied. "But something is not right about all of this. I can't put my finger on it."

"Nothing is right down here," said Jake, exasperated. "Come on, you guys! I bet it won't take us more than five minutes to get to the other side."

He began to walk down the path. After only ten yards, however, he halted so abruptly that Miranda bumped into him, causing Pablo to squeak angrily. Jake pointed up at one of the trees. "What the heck is *that?*"

An enormous web hung across the cement path between two umdhlebi trees, like a dirty white sheet on a clothesline. It looked thick and cottony, like one of those fake Halloween spider webs. It stretched from the top branches of the trees all the way to the ground.

"That is the nastiest web I've ever seen," said Miranda anxiously. She hated spiders with a passion. "What kind of spider makes webs this big?"

Cazador examined the web and glanced about the chamber. "Only one species is capable of such webs," he said. "The *j'ba fosi*, also known as the Congolese giant spider. It's one of the most feared cryptids in the deep forests of the Congo. We must proceed very cautiously."

"When you say *giant*," began Miranda. "You mean for a spider, right?"

"No, I mean *giant*," the doctor replied. "The j'ba fosi have seven-foot-long legs and a cephalothorax and abdomen as big as a kitchen table. They're clever, too." He pointed his machete at the web. "But this chamber is a long way from their original enclosure. There's no source of food for them here. Unless—" His eyes suddenly went wide. "We need to turn back. We're not safe here. Perhaps we can move the rubble away from the service corridor."

"I have a better idea," said Jake. "One that doesn't involve heading back toward Bolo and those huge crocodile things." He grabbed the flashlight from Miranda's hand and stepped off the walkway, walking quickly around a web toward an opening between it and an umdhlebi tree. "Follow me."

"No, Jake!" shouted Cazador. "Don't leave the path! What are you doing?"

"Don't be ridiculous, Jake!" yelled Miranda. "Are you trying to get yourself killed?"

He glanced back at them. "Relax," he said. "I'm going to find us a shortcut. Sometimes it takes an outside-the-box tyro such as myself to—"

And then the cave floor seemed to give way beneath him and he fell downward into darkness.

29

Down the Spider Hole

Jake always imagined that there were two kinds of people in the world: those who are afraid of spiders and those who aren't. He assumed that he was in the latter category. He didn't mind spiders. Or at least he didn't *hate* them. And he definitely couldn't remember ever being scared of them in his life, even when he was little.

All that changed when he fell into the j'ba fosi trap. He knew the hidden door must have snapped closed behind him because the absolute darkness of the hole made the dim cavern above seem as bright as a summer day. He heard Miranda and Cazador shouting outside, but their voices were muffled.

He pushed himself up into a sitting position and rubbed his head. He must have bumped it against something during the fall. He knew he had to find the flashlight before he could do anything else. If a humongous spider was sitting next to him, he needed to know right away. He groped blindly around the floor of the pit. It was littered with debris. His hand grabbed something wet and squishy that felt like a mound of Jell-O. Yuck, he thought. Definitely *not* a flashlight. He pushed the panicky feeling down into his stomach and continued to look for the light.

Finally, his left hand closed around a cool metallic object

and he pressed a button. The hole flooded with light. No spiders in sight—giant or otherwise. The cell was only about four feet wide and six feet long, but it was deep. When he stood up, the trapdoor was still two feet above his head. At one end, the space narrowed to a smaller area that was densely thick with cobwebs. That had to be the spider's entrance, he thought. Hopefully, the owner was on vacation.

Carnage lay everywhere. He saw a jawbone that might have once belonged to an amarok. There were a few partial skeletons of smaller animals. He noticed a lumpy object near him encased in webbing. The distinctive spiky backbone of a chupacabra poked through the white gauze. He shuddered. A chupacabra burrito, he thought. And it looked fresh.

He brushed off his pants and pulled a piece of webbing from his hair. Besides the bump on his head, he'd also suffered a cut on his arm. He aimed the flashlight toward the trap door and reached up as high as he could. He could barely touch it with his fingertips. It felt hard. He searched for handholds in the lair's walls, but they were as smooth as glass.

"Jake!" He could barely hear Miranda's muffled voice through the trap door. "Are you OK?"

He banged the end of the flashlight against the trapdoor. It was as sturdy as a manhole cover. "I'm fine! I'd be a lot better if I could find a way out of here."

"Is the spider with you?" yelled Cazador.

For a genius, thought Jake, sometimes the doctor had no common sense. "Yes, a huge, man-eating spider is sitting right next to me," he replied sarcastically. "Do you want me to say hi for you?"

"If it's not there yet, it will be soon," replied Cazador, ignoring his sarcasm. "Hurry! There's no time for dilly-dallying."

What did he think he was doing down here? thought Jake. Checking email? "I can't find a step ladder, doctor," he said. "I think the spider forgot to leave one."

Despite his attempts at humor, Jake started to get nervous. The spider designed the trap to keep prey from escaping, and that's exactly what it was doing. He had a bad feeling that the owner of the trap would soon be back to see what she'd caught.

"Stand back, Jake!" yelled Miranda. "Cazador is going to chop through the door with the machete."

Above him, he heard the loud thump of a machete against the trapdoor. Particles of dust drifted down through the flashlight's beam. As he swept the beam around the cell, Jake thought he saw eight, shiny round gems glinting through the dirt-encrusted web at the far end of the hole. The gems were in a row, like amber-tinted jewels on a necklace.

Fear suddenly seized him. Those weren't jewels, he thought. They were yellow, golf-ball-sized *spider* eyes. He swallowed hard and stumbled backward. He was about to come face to face with a spider as big as a cow.

"Uh, Cazador," he stammered. "I think the j'ba fosi just showed up. Do you have a really, *really* big shoe? Actually, maybe a baseball bat would work better."

"Listen, Jake!" shouted the doctor. "Get as far away from the trap door as you can. Find a corner and dig yourself in. Understand?"

"Got it!" Jake backed up against the far wall. He pointed his light up at the ceiling and saw the trap door clearly outlined against the dark black rock. "Whatever you're going to do, you better do it fast."

In the silence, he heard a soft crunching sound, like some-one walking on dry grass. He pointed the flashlight in the di-rection of the noise. The j'ba fosi had emerged from its tunnel now and was moving toward him. The spider was truly enor-mous. It was covered in brown fur and had legs as thick as logs. Its eight eyes were arranged bizarrely in the center of its monstrous head, with four in one row and another four above. Pincers protruded from its mouth. Suddenly, he felt like a per-son that just realized he's swimming with a great white shark.

But the spider stopped when Jake shined the flashlight on it. After a few seconds, it began to creep toward him again.

Then the world seemed to explode. Jake heard a booming noise as dirt, rock, bones, and pieces of trapdoor flew in every direction. When he opened his eyes again, he aimed the flash-light at a large mound in front of him, which now consisted of the remains of the trap door, a hundred pounds of rock, and one Congolese giant spider underneath it all.

Cazador stood on top of the entire heap, a satisfied grin on his face.

"Dr. Jorge Isidoro de San Luis Cazador, at your service!" he announced grandly. "Are you ready to leave? What am I say-ing? We *must* leave now! *Ándale!*" He paused, glancing around the cell. "By the way, where is the j'ba fosi?"

"You're standing on her," said Jake, spitting out dust and who-knows-what from his mouth.

"Am I?" He looked down doubtfully. A few of the spider's hairy legs were visible beneath the rubble. "Is she dead?"

As if the spider had been listening, it shifted and squirmed, causing Cazador almost to lose his balance.

"I think that would be a 'no,'" Jake replied.

"I believe you're correct," the doctor said. "Let me help you out of here."

Jake stood up and climbed carefully on top of the pile. "You're the one with the bad leg," he said. "You go first. I'll help you up."

He hooked his hands together so that Cazador could put his foot in. He lifted him up until the old man's hands found the edge of the pit. Finally, his legs were clear of the hole.

Miranda's head appeared above the pit. "Anytime now, Jake."

He looked down at the j'ba fosi below him. It seemed to be growing angrier the more it struggled to get out from beneath the debris. Jake felt as if he were on a boat during a storm at sea. "I'll be right back," he said, jumping down from the mound of rubble. "Make room for me up there!"

"What are you doing?" asked Miranda, her voice rising.

He walked to the end of the cell. With a running start, he jumped onto the pile just as the spider pulled itself loose of the rubble. As he'd hoped, the beast's spongy body provided just enough lift to propel him upward like a trampoline. He reached up and Cazador and Miranda caught his arms and dragged him out. The three of them half-crawled, half-ran away from the pit.

After he'd caught his breath, Jake sat up. "Sorry about that," he said. "Maybe that wasn't such a great short cut after all."

Cazador pulled a chunk of spider trap-door from Jake's backpack. "That is the understatement of the century, *mi hijo*," he said. "But you gave your sister an idea. Tell him your plan, *señorita*."

Miranda pointed to the j'ba fosi webs. "The spiders put

webs across the path to force careless prey—that would be you, Jake—off the cement pathway," she explained. "That's because they can't dig their traps in the cement. So as long as we stay on the cement path, we should be fine."

"But how do we get past the webs?" asked Jake.

"You're going to hack us a path through them," Cazador said, handing him the rusty machete.

Miranda grinned. "We figure that's the least you can do for us rescuing you."

Somewhere in the corridor behind them, they heard the faint but unmistakable howl of an amarok. Jake took the machete and gave it a couple of practice swings. It felt good in his hands.

"What are we waiting for?" he said. "Let's whack some webs!"

30

Domain of the Death Worm

A fter his near-death experience in the j'ba fosi pit, Jake took great pleasure in chopping through the webs. As he grunted and flailed away with the machete, Miranda and Cazador scanned the umdhlebi trees along the walkway for spiders.

"We can't see them, but they're all around us—hundreds of them," said Cazador, glancing down at the crypticon, which emitted a constant series of low beeps. "We should be grateful that there's light in this enclosure. If it were any darker, we'd be overrun by now."

The thought of even one j'ba fosi now gave Jake a serious case of the creeps. He couldn't even imagine being chased by *hundreds* of them.

"Can't you go any faster, Jake?" asked Miranda. She still carried Pablo, who had strands of webbing in his golden fur. "Cazador's pep talks aren't very peppy."

"I agree," said Jake between swings. "But I'm going as fast as I can. This isn't as easy as it looks."

At last, they stood in front of the opening of the tunnel on the other side of the chamber. The steel door had been ripped from its hinges and lay among the umdhlebi.

"What kind of cryptid can do *that?*" Jake asked, wiping

sweat from his forehead.

Cazador limped past him into the tunnel. "I can think of three off the top of my head," he remarked. "Do you need to know their names right now or can it wait?"

"It can wait," mumbled Jake.

They followed the doctor down the dark corridor. After a while, the cut on Jake's arm started bleeding again. They stopped while Miranda found bandages and bacterial ointment in the backpack. They had a sip of water from their remaining canteen of water. Miranda's khaki uniform was grimy with dirt and one of her sleeves was completely ripped away. She looked pale and exhausted, but Jake assumed he looked even worse. His entire body ached and he kept finding pieces of spider debris in his clothes.

Miranda gave him a weak smile. "Do you think we'll ever get out of here?"

"We'd better," replied Jake. "This place is hazardous to our health." He glanced over at Cazador, who was examining the map he'd torn out of the bestiary. "How far to that secret exit door, Cazador?"

"We're only two chambers away," he replied. "With any luck, we can avoid these areas here and here." He tapped the map with his finger. "That will put us right by Lost Lake. From there, the service entrance is very close."

"I wonder where Bolo and his men are," said Miranda. "Not that I'm complaining, but shouldn't they have caught up to us by now?"

The doctor folded up the map and stood up. "I imagine they have their hands full," he said. "Remember—they don't have a crypticon or a map. In fact, we're actually lucky that

Markus sent them after us."

Jake frowned. "Don't we have enough trouble down here with the cryptids without a bunch of human psychopaths chasing us?"

"If not for Bolo and his men, we'd be the center of attention," replied Cazador. "As it stands, the cryptids are much more interested in them than us."

Jake put the backpack back on. "Let's hope it stays that way," he said. "By the way, which cryptids *haven't* we met yet?"

"Quite a few, actually," the doctor replied as they began to walk. "For example, we haven't seen any Ethiopian death birds or a culebrón. And don't forget the yacumama."

"Maybe it didn't survive," said Miranda, shining the flashlight on the pathway in front of them. "If it's that big, it would need a lot of food. Maybe they all starved to death."

He shook his head. "I don't think so. As with most large snakes, the yacumama only needs to eat a few times a year. It could survive as long as it caught a mahamba or a couple of careless chupacabras now and then."

"Or a few humans," added Jake. "Just throwing that out there."

They heard a sudden outburst of yips and barks behind them, followed closely by the pop-pop-pop of gunfire. Bolo were catching up to them. Pablo burrowed himself into Miranda's neck, squeezing his eyes shut. "Don't worry, Pablo," she said. "Nobody's going to get you while I'm here."

Cazador peered down the corridor and frowned. "We need to pick up our pace," he said. "The next chamber should be the final one before we reach the lake. The map doesn't indicate which cryptid we put there, but I'm sure it will come to me."

Despite his worsening limp, the doctor marched forward relentlessly. After climbing up a long staircase that had been cut into the rock wall, they entered into another dimly lighted chamber. It was about the size of the umdhlebi enclosure. The floor was flat, with the exception of a few dozen earthen mounds the size of speed bumps scattered throughout the cave. Large rocks had fallen off the walls around the cave's perimeter. Down the middle of the cave, from one entrance to the other, ran a cracked and badly eroded cement pathway.

Cazador shook his head in dismay. "I just remembered which cryptid lives in this enclosure. What a disaster!"

"What are you talking about?" asked Jake, looking around the cave. "It's completely empty, except for all those piles of dirt."

"Those piles are considerably more dangerous than you realize, Jake," said Cazador. He turned to Miranda. "Before your brother tries to get himself killed again, remind him of the fourth law of cryptozoology."

"Gladly, doctor," she said. "It's the cryptid you *don't* see that is the most dangerous one of all."

"*Exactamente,*" said Cazador. "And it just so happens that the unseen cryptid in this enclosure can kill us as quickly as a mahamba."

"I wasn't just going sprint over to the other side, you guys," said Jake. "Give me a little credit." He had to admit that his first instinct was to do exactly that. Compared to the other caverns they'd seen, this one seemed harmless. "But I don't get it. There's nothing here."

Cazador removed the crypticon from his pocket and turned it on. He sighed and sat down on nearby rock. "I would never have imagined there could be so many after all these years," he said, showing them the crypticon. Dozens of green dots filled the screen. "Look at them. They're everywhere!"

Miranda sat down beside him with Pablo. "What is everywhere, doctor? What cryptid are you talking about?"

"The *olgoi khorkhoi*." He spat out the words with disgust. "The Mongolian Death Worm. I believe that my former security director and current tormentor mentioned them to you on your first day at the zoo. Markus and Feng must have told him about the animals of the Underzoo."

Miranda's eyes widened. "When we were looking through the bestiary near the aquarium, we saw a few photos of them," she said. "They're sort of big slugs that live underground. Are those mounds of dirt where the worm has emerged?"

"Those aren't mounds of dirt," said Cazador. "They're the death worm's victims—former residents of the Underzoo. They're the remains of animals that have tried to cross this chamber. As you can see from the crypticon, the *olgoi khorkhoi* have colonized the whole cave. It's a mine field out there."

For Jake, the cave's temperature suddenly seemed to go up by twenty degrees. Almost as warm as the digestive track of a prehistoric killer cryptid, he thought. "How do the worms catch their victims?" he asked. "Do they burst out of the soil or something?"

The doctor shook his head. "Nothing so dramatic. The worm's methods of hunting are more sinister."

"Oh, no," exclaimed Jake. "Not more trapdoors! I don't think I can take any more of those."

The doctor gazed out over the chamber. "No trapdoors. They don't need them. We found this colony by accident in

1996 when one of our native guides collapsed outside a village in northern Mongolia on the outskirts of the Gobi Desert. He died before he hit the ground. When we managed to bring back some of the worms to the Z.I.A., one of my most experienced zookeepers died inside the worm enclosure. As best we can tell, the worms kill using an electrical impulse. After the last keeper passed way, I moved the worms down here. I remember one occasion—"

"No offense, doctor," interrupted Miranda. "But maybe now isn't the time for stories. If we don't get to the other side of this chamber soon, Bolo or whatever is chasing him is going to catch up."

"She's right, doctor," said Jake. "We need to get through this chamber quickly. Let's just follow the cement pathway like we did in the j'ba fosi enclosure."

"That won't work," said Cazador forlornly. "Look at the distribution of the corpses. A few are right in right the middle of the walkway. I don't think it's any safer than the dirt. We might be better off taking our chances with Bolo and his mercenaries."

"There must be a better option than that," said Jake. He wracked his brain for a solution. Stilts? Jet packs? Skipping extra fast? No, no, and *definitely* no. "Bolo is going to be even angrier now that he's had to fight all those cryptids. And he started out in a bad mood."

Suddenly, Pablo climbed down Miranda's arm and darted into the shadows along the cave wall to their right.

"No, Pablo!" shouted Miranda. "Come back! It's not safe!"

In the dim light, they watched as the tiny monkey scrambled along a barely visible rocky path near the base of the wall.

He avoided touching the cave floor, springing effortlessly from rock to rock.

"I think he knows what he's doing," murmured Miranda.

"I can't believe it!" Jake exclaimed. "He's showing us a way through the chamber. And this whole time I thought he was just lazy."

"He's not lazy," she said defensively. "He just doesn't like walking. He's got little legs."

"But how did he know about the worms?" asked Jake.

Cazador stood up and put the crypticon back in his jacket pocket. "Who knows?" he said. "Ink monkeys have served humans for hundreds of years. Granted, most of the time they were simply helping ancient Chinese scholars with their manuscripts—fetching pens, turning pages, and so on. But perhaps Pablo senses the hidden dangers in the chamber. In any case, we'd better follow him, don't you think?"

With Cazador leading the way, they began to creep along the cave wall. "Be careful!" he said. "If you step onto the dirt floor, it could be as fatal as falling off a cliff." When they'd reached the half-way point, the doctor stopped. "There it is," he whispered. "The *olgoi khorkhoi*."

Less than ten yards away, they saw a two-foot-long blood-colored log as thick as a person's arm. Its moist, leathery skin was a deep crimson color, with blotches of black scattered over its body. Jake couldn't tell which end was which, though it seemed to be feeding on a dead amarok. As it ate, its body pulsated and quivered. It was the most disgusting thing he'd ever seen.

"It's rare to see them above ground," remarked Cazador. "Be vigilant here. Death worms are capable of squirting lethally corrosive venom, but only when threatened."

They continued to skirt the wall, stepping gingerly along the ledge. Jake almost lost his balance once or twice, but he caught himself in time. At last they reached the back wall, walking the final twenty yards across the rocks until they stood at the raised area in front of the tunnel on the other side of the cave. Pablo greeted Miranda by climbing up her leg and onto her shoulder.

"You saved our lives, you weird little monkey," she said, giving him a hug. "You deserve a special treat." She removed a pen from her pocket and gave it to him. He snatched it and cracked it in two, sucking on it like a candy cane.

Movement on the other side of the chamber caught Jake's eye. He squinted across the enclosure's ghostly landscape. "Guys," he whispered. "Do you notice anything strange over there by the tunnel?"

Cazador looked up. "Get down!" he shouted in alarm.

They threw themselves to the ground as yellow muzzle flashes burst from the darkness, accompanied by deafening blasts from high caliber rifles.

31

The Fatal Backpack

It felt like an entire army had invaded the chamber. Miranda and Jake dropped to their stomachs as bullets whizzed past them into the rock wall, sending down a cascade of stone and dirt upon them. From the corner of his eye, Jake saw Cazador tumble backwards, hitting his head on a small boulder. Jake and Miranda huddled together on the ground, trying to protect their faces from the flying debris.

"Stop! We give up!" screamed Jake, daring to glance up for a moment. "Knock it off! STOP SHOOTING!"

The gunfire ceased. A layer of smoke hovered over the cave and the air felt thick with the sour smell of sulphur. Jake and Miranda rose slowly to their feet. They glanced over at Cazador. He was lying unconscious on the ground. Pablo crouched next to him, whimpering.

Bolo Young, followed by four of his men, emerged from the tunnel across the chamber. Two of the men carried automatic rifles. One of them had a streak of dried blood on his face with a bandage wrapped around his shoulder. They looked like they had been in a war. Bolo adjusted his rifle on his shoulder and smirked.

"Y'all don't know what we've been through to get here," he yelled. "Two of my men quit after those giant crocs attacked us. Another one got sliced up pretty bad by one of those mutant wolves. Jericho went missing somewhere in that enclosure with those nasty trees. I don't know how the three of you made it this far, but it ends now."

Jake looked over at Miranda. "What should we do?" he whispered.

"I don't know," she said. "We need Cazador to wake up. We can't drag him all the way to the lake."

Jake thought about it. "I have an idea. It's a long shot, but it might buy us some time."

"All right," she said. "But try not to get killed."

"You finally did it, Bolo," yelled Jake, pointing at the unconscious Cazador. "You killed him. You can go back and tell Alaweed and the professor the news. I'm sure you'll get a pat on the head."

"Here's the deal, kid," said Bolo. "We don't have a problem with you or your sister. And I don't care if the doc's dead or not. In fact, I personally like y'all—you got guts. But I need that crypticon. If you bring it over here, my boys and I will leave you alone." He grinned maliciously. "At least until the critters come for you. Then you'll have *plenty* of company."

Jake shook his head. "Don't you know where we are right now? This is the Mongolian death worm chamber. You were the one who told us about them, so you must know what they can do. They're underground, waiting for you to do something stupid."

Bolo exchanged a glance with his companions. "Nice try, kid," he said. "Becker already told us they're hibernating. Those worms are about as deadly as gophers right now. You made it over there, didn't you?"

Jake's stomach sank. Was Cazador wrong about the death worms? Or did Professor Becker lie to Bolo? "Well, we're still not bringing the crypticon over to you. But I'll throw it over to you with the backpack. It's been nothing but trouble for us anyway."

Before Bolo could say anything, Jake heaved the pack as far as he could. It landed near the cement walkway, about half-way across the chamber. Bolo glowered at him nastily, but Jake didn't look away. "If you want it so bad, you can go get it," he said. "But I wouldn't try it if I were you. Cazador didn't mention anything about hibernation. I'd say those things are as deadly as ever."

Miranda gaped at Jake as if he'd gone crazy. "What are you doing? We can't give them the crypticon! You know what Ala-weed will do with it. Besides, we need it to get out of here."

"Don't worry," he whispered. "It's in Cazador's jacket. I'm hoping this gets them to give up and go home."

They heard a groan behind them. Miranda ran over to Cazador and knelt beside him. "He's waking up! He has a nasty bump on the back of his head, but otherwise he looks all right."

Jake was focusing on the men across the cave. They were huddled together like football players planning their next play. "See if you can get him on his feet," he told her. "We might have to get out of here in a hurry."

At last, Bolo turned back to face them. He stared greedily out at the backpack. "Not smart, kid," he shouted. "Carlos is coming over to get the crypticon. After that, he's going to take care of the three of you. Seems like the doctor ain't as dead as you thought."

Jake felt a flutter of panic. He didn't think "taking care of them" meant handing out bags of candy and escorting them back to the Z.I.A.

"You don't know what you're doing, Bolo!" Miranda shouted. "Cazador showed us the worms on the crypticon. Look at all the dead animals! Just turn around and nobody else will get hurt."

But the man named Carlos was already making his way across the chamber along the cement path. Whenever he came to a carcass, he carefully stepped over it. Within a minute, he had reached the backpack. He stooped down and picked it up. "I got it," he yelled over to Bolo. "You want me to bring it back right now?"

"Just toss it over here," replied Bolo. "Then go deal with Cazador and the two brats. And hurry up! I want to get out of this stink hole."

Carlos heaved the backpack to Bolo and the remaining two men. One of them caught it in midair. Then he looked over at Jake and Miranda with what could have been pity.

"It's just not your day," he said, shaking his head. "Oh, well. It's not my problem." He began to walk toward them.

Cazador was now on his feet, looking unsteady. Pablo sat on one of his shoulders, his tiny hands clasping the doctor's silver hair. "What is that man doing?" he asked. "Is he insane?"

Miranda sighed. "He might be insane, doctor, but he's still alive. Bolo said the worms are hibernating. That guy is walking over here to kill us."

"That's absurd!" exclaimed Cazador scornfully. "Death worms don't hibernate. Young man, turn around and go back to your friends right now if you want to live!"

Ten yards away, Carlos stopped in mid-stride as if obeying Cazador's command. His body became as stiff as a mannequin. His mocking grin was gone, replaced by a rigid mask of terror. From his left eye, a single drop of blood ran down his cheek, like a scarlet tear. Then, like a statue falling off its pedestal, he pitched forward onto the cave floor and lay still.

"Too late," said Cazador sadly.

Bolo and the two remaining mercenaries stared in horror at the fallen man. Then they began arguing loudly with one another.

"Let's get out of here," whispered Jake.

They slipped into the tunnel and walked swiftly away from the enclosure. The path immediately began to slope downward, growing warmer and wetter the farther down they went. Cazador removed the crypticon from his pocket. "No cryptids in our immediate vicinity so far," he said, staring down at the screen. "That will change once we get to Lost Lake."

After another fifteen minutes of hiking, the tunnel opened up into a vast chamber. The scent of water and animal manure grew more intense. Miranda shined her flashlight at the ceiling of the cave. The ceiling was studded with stalactites and other bizarre rock formations.

"Point the light out there," said Cazador. "Straight ahead."

Miranda aimed the flashlight over the water. The light revealed a black lake that stretched in every direction as far as they could see. It was still and smooth, like a pool of liquid glass. She knelt down and dipped her hand in the water. "It's warm," she said. "There must be a hot springs down here, right?"

"Several hot springs feed Lost Lake," he said. "Yet another fortuitous aspect that made these mines an ideal location for the Underzoo."

"Are you sure there are cryptids in this cavern?" asked Jake. "I sort of hoped they'd be taking a nap or—I don't know— dead."

The doctor arched one of his furry eyebrows. "Unlikely. As I told you, Lost Lake will be the gathering spot for most of the cryptids in the Underzoo. It's like a seasonal pond in the African savannah."

They stepped onto a crumbling brick path lined with rusty, three-foot-high wrought-iron posts strung with metal cable. Cazador pressed a button on the crypticon. As the device flickered to life, they waited anxiously for the beeps and swarming pixels that would tell them that they were about to be bitten, trampled, or eaten. This time the screen remained dark and the device was silent.

"Well, *that's* good news," said Miranda, relieved. "That means no cryptids, right?"

"Not yet, anyway," said Cazador. "But keep your eyes and ears open. This way."

The doctor stepped over the metal rope beside the path and strode away from the lake. When they caught up with him, he was standing in front of a giant boulder the size of a small house. "This is the control room," he said. "We designed it to resemble one of the boulders. Let's hope it still works. Without light, we'll never find our way across this chamber."

He slid up a panel embedded into the rock and punched in a code. They heard a loud click. He pushed the heavy door inward. Miranda shined the flashlight inside. The control room was the size of a classroom, with computers and keyboards on various tables. Buttons, levers, and fuse boxes lined the walls.

A layer of dust blanketed everything.

"By now, Bolo must know we're heading for Lost Lake," Cazador explained. "It won't take him long to figure out that there is another way out of the Underzoo. We need to move quickly before he find's Pablo's trail through the olgoi khorkhoi chamber." He limped over to several large levers on the wall, pushing up each one. Then he pressed a button on one of the machines on the table. Lights appeared and the computer began to hum. "That should do it. Let's go see how Lost Lake has fared after ten years of neglect."

32

Terror from Above

As they exited the control room, they gazed in wonder at the cave's transformation.

Hundreds of lights shimmered throughout the cavern. They were placed along the path and on tall posts around the lake. There were dozens inserted into the cave's ceiling, like stars in the night sky. There were even lights under the water near the shore that shined up through the lake. Even Pablo seemed impressed, his eyes twinkling as he surveyed the chamber.

"This might be the most beautiful place I've ever seen in my life," said Miranda.

"It's fantastic," agreed Jake. "It must have taken you forever to build it."

The doctor nodded. "I spared no expense on this section of the cave. Lost Lake should have been the crown jewel of the Underzoo. Unfortunately, the cryptids had other plans."

Suddenly, the crypticon erupted in a flurry of angry beeps. Blue dots danced at the edge of the screen. Cazador burst into a long series of angry-sounding Spanish words. "More bad news, I'm afraid," he said. He looked to his right where the lake disappeared around a tall rock formation in the distance. "A pack of lemischi is heading this way. We're exposed here.

We need to find a boat."

"A boat?" asked Miranda as they moved quickly over toward the dock. "I thought we were taking the trail around the lake."

"Who cares at this point?" asked Jake, who knew his sister hated lakes, oceans, or anything else with deeper water than her bathtub. "The real question is: What in the world is a lemischi? Are they like lemmings? Because I'm pretty sure I could handle a lemming."

"Unfortunately, they're nothing like lemmings," said Cazador, worriedly. "*Lemischi* is their name in Tehuelche. Others call them Patagonian water tigers. They resemble giant ground sloths, but they act more like grizzly bears. Right now, at least five are heading our way on the path." He pointed across the lake. "See those lights going up the wall?" They peered across the lake. Lights angled steeply from the cave floor along the distant wall toward the ceiling. "Those mark the trail that leads to the service entrance. Unless we want to swim there, we have to locate a boat."

They walked over to a cement dock that jutted thirty feet into the lake. There were some old ropes tied to it that had rotted away and were now hanging limply in the water. A few oars were scattered haphazardly on the dock. They saw the remains of two boats half-submerged in the water.

This was going to be a long, wet trip, thought Jake.

"There's a boat!" shouted Miranda, pointing to a narrow beach to the left of the dock. "Over there on the beach. I think it's in one piece."

They found a white, wooden rowboat lying upside down on the shore. It was twelve feet long and had thin black stripes running down each side.

"I don't see any holes in it," said Cazador. "Let's put it in the water and see if it floats."

Together, they turned the boat over and pushed it onto the lake. Jake felt his shoes fill with warm water.

"No leaks," said Miranda, looking into the boat's hull. "But are you sure we can't take the trail? I'm not a good swimmer. At all."

A loud, rumbling growl echoed through the chamber. The doctor glanced down at the crypticon. "There's no time, Miranda. The lemischi are coming up the path from the north. If we meet them on the trail…"

His voice trailed off, as if he couldn't even imagine such a terrible fate.

They helped Miranda into the boat, handing her two oars. Pablo clung to her shoulder as usual, looking anxious. Cazador eased himself over the gunnel. The boat rocked unsteadily. Jake waded deeper into the water and lifted himself into the boat. As he tried to sit down, he lost his balance. Cazador grabbed his legs, steadying him. "Careful, *hijo*," he said. "There's no time for a swim right now."

Jake sat down and picked up two of the oars. He slid them into the metal brackets on the edge of the boat and began to row.

"Once we're out on the lake, my only concern is a yacumama," said the doctor. "If the lights don't attract it, the smell of food certainly will. Try not to touch the water with your skin or make too much noise." It took Jake a second to realize that "food" meant them. "I'll keep an eye on the crypticon," Cazador continued. "You row, Jake—enthusiastically, if you don't mind. The faster we get across this lake, the better."

As he rowed, Jake thought about how desperate their situation was. If they capsized, he doubted that they could make it back to shore. Cazador would be lucky to last a minute with his injured leg. The terrified expression on Miranda's face told him that she'd need a lot of help as well. He swam well, but the cut he'd received from falling into the j'ba fosi pit made his right leg ache painfully.

His thoughts were interrupted by the now-familiar sound of gunfire. They looked toward the dock in time to see Bolo and his two companions burst out of the tunnel, slipping and stumbling on the brick path. A few seconds later, a pack of chupacabras poured into the cave in hot pursuit. One of the men fired a shot at the snarling animals before following Bolo onto the dock. At the other end of the cavern, dark shapes oozed out of the darkness, lumbering toward the commotion of men and animals near the dock.

"Here come the lemischi," said Cazador grimly. "With any luck, they'll keep Bolo and his companions occupied until we're safely on the other side."

Jake saw the huge animals perfectly now. As the doctor had promised, the lemischi were frightening—as large as bears, but with arms as long as those of apes, with knives for claws. They did look a little like giant sloths. Unlike sloths, however, they weren't hunting for leaves and berries to eat. Bolo and his men had no clue that their situation was about to get much worse.

"Hey, Bolo!" shouted Miranda suddenly. She pointed in the direction of the lemischi. "Behind you!"

Bolo looked up from the chupacabra he was fighting and peered out at the water. Then he whirled around to defend himself against the lemischi.

Jake almost dropped his oars in astonishment. "What are you doing, Miranda?" he hissed. "Those are the bad guys, remember? Why are you helping them? The lemischi are on *our* team right now."

"Those things will rip them limb from limb," she said defiantly. "No one deserves to die like that. Not even Bolo."

Jake glared at her. "Great! Now they can keep on hunting us with all their limbs intact. I can't believe—"

"She's right, Jake," interrupted Cazador. He looked at Miranda and smiled. "Your sister is reminding us of our humanity. We should never lower ourselves to the level of our enemies. If we do, we're no better than beasts." He looked apprehensively at the opposite shore. "Speaking of beasts, I would suggest that you row faster, Jake."

Bolo and his men had retreated toward the beach, wading into the water to try to escape the cryptids. Luckily for them, the lemischi and the chupacabras were now locked in a ferocious battle with each other and paid no attention to them.

"Is there anything new on the crypticon, doctor?" asked Miranda.

Cazador looked down at the device. "Yes, there are new cryptids appearing," he said. He pointed to the south. "They're coming from over there."

"What are they?" asked Jake.

"It's hard to tell," replied the doctor. "The screen shows all the colors of a rainbow. A herd of mahambas is swimming along the shore from the south and four amaroks are approaching from the north, probably tracking the lemischi. At least the eastern shore is clear. That's where we're heading.

Wait a minute." He paused. "Oh, no. This isn't good at all."

"What now?" Miranda and Jake blurted out at once.

"It's a yacumama," he said gravely. "And it's heading our way."

Jake stopped rowing for a moment. "You mean that giant snake?"

"That's the one," he replied. "But they're slow swimmers. With any luck, we'll be on shore before it gets here. Keep rowing."

The noise in the cave became deafening. There were growls, roars, even occasional screams coming from the cryptid brawl. As he rowed, Jake saw a lemisch seize one of the chupacabras in its claws and hurl it into the lake. The amaroks had arrived and were starting to tear into both packs. It was like a scene from a horror movie.

"There's Bolo!" exclaimed Miranda. "Oh, rats. He found a boat."

Jake strained his eyes to see through the dim light of the cave. Sure enough, the three men were struggling to climb into a boat identical to their own.

"I don't think they have any oars," said Miranda. "As long as we keep rowing, we should be able to—" She stopped suddenly and pointed at the ceiling. "What in the world is *that?*"

They glanced up. Something enormous was flying toward them. It was bigger than any bird, with a wingspan as long as their boat. Its feathers were jet black and its beak looked sharper than a razor. It bore down on them, extending its talons like coiled springs.

Cazador jumped to his feet so quickly that he dropped the crypticon into the boat's hold. He grabbed one of the oars and began waving it madly in the air. "Get back, *diablo!*" he yelled. "Back, I say!" The beating of the bird's wings as it descended caused a mini-whirlwind that pitched the boat to and fro, nearly catapulting all of them into the water. Jake and Miranda covered their heads with their arms. When they looked up again, the bird had disappeared.

And so had Cazador.

Pablo squeaked fearfully, desperately clutching Miranda's arm. They scanned the lake in every direction. No Cazador, no bird, no anything.

What were they supposed to do now? thought Jake. They were in the middle of a lake, being chased by three homicidal humans and a dozen lethal cryptids—including a sixty-foot snake that could swallow their boat whole. And the only person who could help them had just been kidnapped by a giant bird with *serious* anger-management issues.

33

Bolo's Final Shot

"W hat *was* that?" exclaimed Jake when he'd recovered from his shock. "And has it done with Dr. Cazador?"

"I don't know," said Miranda. Her clothes were soaked with lake water. Pablo was also drenched. He whined pitifully as he clung to her arm. "I didn't see anything after he jumped up and started swinging that oar. He saved our lives, Jake."

"And now he's gone," said Jake, picking up the crypticon from the bottom of the boat. Behind them they could hear Bolo and his men splashing and yelling. They were getting closes. "Where's the other oar?"

"I don't know," she said, glancing around the boat. "It must have fallen into the lake when that bird attacked us."

Jake took the remaining oar from its bracket and handed her the crypticon. "I'll row. You keep an eye out for that snake." He took a final look into the dark recesses of the cave and shuddered. Nobody could have survived that demon bird, he thought. Not even Cazador.

But they had no time to mourn. On shore, the epic cryptid brawl grew even more chaotic. The chupacabras and amaroks were forcing the lemischi into the lake. Another pack of animals arrived from the south. As Miranda studied the crypticon, he rowed as fast as he could with only one oar. What would they do when they found the back entrance? he wondered. If it was like the other doors in the cave, it wouldn't open without a code.

Without Cazador, their odds of making it out of the Underzoo had gone from low to zilch.

"Not to freak you out or anything, Jake," said Miranda anxiously. "But Bolo's getting closer. Can you row any faster?"

"I'm trying," he said between strokes. "This is even harder than hacking through those spider webs." He didn't need her to tell him how close Bolo was. In another minute, Bolo would be able to tell him himself. "Do you see any signs of that yacumama yet?"

"I'm not sure what all these dots stand for," she replied, frowning at the crypticon. "What color did he say the snake's dot was?"

"I don't think he told us," he said. "But he said it would be coming from the east."

Her eyes peered across the dark lake. "There's only one orange dot on this screen, and it's definitely coming from the east." She paused. "It's *really* close, Jake. Maybe less than a minute."

Jake could see the three men in the other boat clearly now. Bolo kept yelling something, but the racket from the cryptids on shore made it impossible to hear what he was saying. Just then, he felt the bottom of the boat scrape against something hard. He looked over his shoulder and saw the brick path snaking up the cave wall. They had made it to the other side of the lake.

Ignoring the pain in his injured leg, he pushed himself out

of the boat. "Quick!" he shouted. "Grab Pablo and let's get out of here!" His feet met solid ground a couple of feet below the surface. He grabbed the front of the boat and dragged it onto the rocky beach. He helped Miranda out of the boat and onto the shore. They began to scramble away from the water.

Suddenly, a thunderous blast boomed behind them, pitching them forward onto their stomachs. Sand, mud, and bits of rock rained down upon their heads. "Hold it right there," yelled Bolo menacingly. "I ain't firing any more warning shots. Now turn around real slow."

Jake and Miranda sat up and turned to face their pursuer. Bolo was sitting in the middle of his boat less than twenty feet away. A man in front was balancing a shotgun on the bow. The boat bobbed gently in the water.

"One more step and Crank here turns you both into cryptid chow," said Bolo. "I don't care if it means blasting that crypticon into a million pieces." He squinted into the darkness. "Where's Cazador?"

"He's gone," said Miranda. "Some huge bird grabbed him and flew off. We don't know where he is—not that you would care."

Bolo's eyes opened wide with surprise. "He got eaten by one of his own pets? That's the best news I've heard in a week. Crazy coot—serves him right." He turned to the big man seated in the rear of the boat. "Well, what are you waiting for? Let's get that crypticon." The man in back nodded. He put his hand in the water and began to paddle.

And then it was as if a powerful geyser suddenly exploded just beneath the boat, catapulting the rowboat with the three men in it twenty feet into the air. As water rained down on Miranda and Jake, they saw that the geyser was actually a giant snake rising out of the lake, pushing the boat above its head like a seal with a ball. The snake's skin was the color of the earth, with brown and black diamond patterns along its side and back. Its body looked as thick as a tree trunk.

When the yacumama reached its full height, it shook its head violently, hurling the men into the lake. Then it sank back into the water and raced toward its prey. Within seconds, it had encircled the men, tightening its massive body around them like a noose. It began to swim away from shore, dragging its victims behind it. With a final shiver, the snake disappeared beneath the slate-colored water, leaving only the splintered remains of the rowboat floating peacefully on the surface.

Miranda and Jake stared out at the lake in horror. They were both soaked to the skin. Pablo shivered on Miranda's lap like a wet ball of yarn.

"That's the worst thing I've ever seen," she said at last. She wiped a tear from her eye. "I wish Cazador were here. How are we ever going to get out of the Underzoo?"

Jake was about to reply when they heard a noise behind them. They turned around in time to see someone limp out of the shadows.

"An excellent question, Miranda," said a familiar voice. "I have a few ideas on the subject."

It was Cazador. He was a mess. His clothes were shredded and covered in dirt. One of his pant legs was entirely gone. He had cuts all over his arms and face and a large black feather stuck out of his silver beard. A piece of egg shell the size of a dinner plate sat on his head. They ran over to him just as he collapsed onto the ground.

"We thought you were dead!" exclaimed Miranda, hugging him tightly as Pablo stroked the doctor's beard. "What the heck is that thing?"

"And where did it take you?" Jake added.

"That is a Thunderbird," said Cazador. "An extremely rare and dangerous animal, originally from the southwestern part of the United States. I should have warned you about her earlier, but both of you seemed anxious enough as it was." He picked the egg shell off his head and tossed it aside. "She's grown a lot in the last ten years. She flew me to her nest, which, thankfully, was on this side of the lake."

"How did you escape?" asked Miranda.

"How did you *live?*" asked Jake.

"I'm not exactly sure," he said. "She flew away immediately after dropping me in her nest. There must be something tastier on the menu than a skinny, old cryptozoologist."

They were quiet for a moment as they stared out at the lake.

"So you met my yacumama?" asked Cazador at last. They nodded. "And Bolo and his men?"

Jake shook his head. "They didn't make it."

The doctor's face grew solemn. "Now you know why I tried to avoid Lost Lake. Did you happen to save the crypticon?"

"We did," said Miranda. "You dropped it in the boat. Here it is."

She handed him the device and he switched it on. The crypticon's screen resembled the sky on Fourth of July. It was full of reds, blues, yellows, oranges, and ten other colors.

Cazador sighed. "It would appear that the entire Underzoo is on its way over to this side of the lake," he remarked calmly. "They must have grown bored fighting each other. We need to get to that exit before they arrive."

Miranda and Jake helped Cazador hike up the narrow path that led up the side of the cave. When they reached the top, they stopped in front of an archway to catch their breath. They stared down at the lake. A mahamba dragged itself onto shore exactly where they'd been sitting a few minutes earlier. It was quickly joined by four others. To their left, they saw three snarling amaroks approach along the trail, eyeing the mahambas warily.

"Round two is about to start," said Jake. "Maybe the yacumama will come back. That would teach those amaroks some manners."

"I'm afraid we'll have to catch the next match," said Cazador. "Hurry—into the tunnel before they see us."

The doctor leaned heavily on them as they walked into the tunnel. He grunted directions as they came to various forks in the corridor. Pale lights along the floor provided some illumination. After several twists and turns, the path ended at a ten-foot-high steel door.

"Finally!" exclaimed Cazador. He turned to them excitedly. "This is it—the back service entrance. I must say, both of you exceeded my wildest expectations. In fact, I hereby promote you to full-fledged keepers. You're no longer tyros." He paused. "This is the part when I would give you a badge and a new uniform. It's really a delightful ceremony."

"Maybe another time, doctor," said Miranda nervously. "At least we now understand why you built the Underzoo. These cryptids shouldn't be allowed *anywhere* near humans."

Jake nodded. "The world may not know it, but it owes you big time."

Cazador's eyes began to water. "Thank you," he said, his voice thick with emotion. "Sometimes it's difficult to remember that my—"

From somewhere behind them, an Amarok howled. "Maybe we should continue this conversation outside," said Jake.

"Agreed," replied the doctor. He slid open the panel and punched in the code. They heard a loud clicking sound as the bolt released. They leaned against the door and pushed with all their strength.

A rush of cool air and sunlight flooded the cave—a magical aroma of pine and sage brush. They walked cautiously through the door, shading their eyes against the sunlight. Cazador shut the door behind them as they squinted about for signs of a hostile welcome party.

They were alone.

They were standing inside a cluster of pines midway up a mountain slope. A gentle breeze teased the tops of the trees. Blue sky shone through the branches like light through the windows of a cathedral.

Midmorning, thought Jake. A new day. After the perilous trip through the Underzoo, it felt more like a new life. He was hungry, thirsty, sore, and utterly exhausted. At the same time, he felt happier than he could ever remember.

But the job wasn't finished. They still had a zoo to save.

34

A Surprise Army

Y ou are absolutely *not* coming with me," said Cazador firmly. "We barely escaped the frying pan and now you want me to throw you into the fire! I won't do it. You must go back home. There's another trail just north of us. Follow it back to Ranchita."

"Not a chance," said Jake. "Besides, Cazador, you can barely walk. You need our help. We're coming with you."

"You *have* to let us help, doctor," said Miranda. "We need to see this through to the end. Anyway, what could Professor Becker do to us that could be worse than throwing us into the Underzoo?"

Cazador pretended to think about it. "Well, let me see," he said. "Oh, I know! *He could shoot you!* In any case, I doubt that Markus and Feng are even in the U.S. anymore. They're probably sipping champagne on one of Alaweed's private yachts even as my cryptids are on their way to his secret zoo."

"Then we can help you clean up the Z.I.A." said Miranda, stroking Pablo, who seemed to be in much better spirits now that he was out of the Underzoo. "Either way, you need us."

Cazador threw up his hands and smiled. "Both of you are as stubborn as emela-ntoukas!" he said. "But the truth is, I *do* need you. If Markus is still here, he'll have his army. But the three of us can't retake the zoo by ourselves. We need help."

"We fought all the cryptids in your Underzoo by ourselves," said Miranda.

"She's right," agreed Jake. "Humans aren't quite as scary once you've been face to face with a j'ba fosi."

"You make a good point," replied the doctor. "Well, let's go take a look at how my zoo is faring under Markus' reign of terror. Then we'll plan our next move."

They found the trail into the main compound and followed it down the hill. After a mile, they stood on a ridge overlooking the hidden valley in which the Z.I.A. was located. At first glance, the zoo seemed unchanged. As they looked more closely, however, they saw that something had changed.

"The doors of the enclosures are open, said Cazador miserably. "They've already taken all the cryptids. We're too late."

"But the place is still swarming with those black-shirted mercenaries," said Jake. "It's seems like nobody has left yet."

Miranda took a few steps to the edge of the trail where it sloped steeply down to the valley floor. She pointed at the road below. "What are all those black trucks doing there?" she asked.

"Trucks?" said Cazador, joining her. "I don't own any black trucks."

Below them were a dozen ominous-looking, semi-trailer trucks parked end to end. Each one was identical—long and black with three vented sky-lights on top. A low rumbling sound indicated that the engines were idling. Six guards with assault rifles loitered near the front of the row of trucks.

"Those are pretty unusual looking trucks," said Jake. "May I see the crypticon for a second, doctor?"

"Of course," said Cazador, handing Jake the device.

Jake turned it on. Immediately, dozens of different colored dots populated the screen and the machine began making the beeping sounds it made when cryptids were nearby. He had no idea which color belonged to which animal, but he knew one thing—there were still lots of cryptids at the zoo.

"They're here!" said Jake excitedly. He showed the screen to Cazador and Miranda. "The cryptids must be in those trucks."

The doctor stared at the crypticon, hardly believing his eyes. *"Maravillosa!"* he exclaimed. "That must be why the trucks have their engines on. They need to power the AC to keep the animals cool."

"If the cryptids are still here," added Miranda, "doesn't that mean the professor will be here as well?"

"You're right," said Cazador, growing excited. "He'd want to stay with his merchandise. In fact, Alaweed would insist on it. We may still have time." He frowned, glancing up at the ridgeline above them as if searching for something. "Now all we need is an army of our own."

More than once that summer, the doctor made them believe he could do magic. Not card tricks or pulling rabbits out of a hat, but *real* magic by a *real* wizard.

This was one of those times.

As they looked up at the ridge, people began to emerge from the forest. The strangers wore camouflage clothing, and a few carried heavy-looking backpacks, long cameras, and rifles. They seemed to have wandered off the set of a Hollywood movie. They marched directly toward them. A very tall man in front of the group grinned and waved.

"Dembi!" exclaimed Miranda. She ran over to the giant

man and threw her arms around him. He leaned down and hugged her. He saw Jake and gave him a thumb's-up sign.

Jake began to recognize other familiar faces: Diana Equinox, Kano Jigaro, Marcelle Bondoc, and Barry Vosloo—all the keepers who had gone to Africa.

Cazador wished for an army and an army appeared.

Cormick saw Jake and winked. "Hiya, laddie," he said. "Can't we leave even for a few days without everything going dead awry? I hope ye didn't get yerself into any mischief whilst we were gone?"

"Just a little," replied Jake, grinning. "Nothing we couldn't handle. Cazador, Miranda and I got to spend some quality time with the cryptids in that *other* zoo you never wanted to talk to me about."

Cormick's face went pale and his eyebrows arched in surprise. "Do you mean to tell me—"

"Welcome back, Cormick!" said Cazador, interrupting him. "What took you so long? I thought you told me that you put a camera near the centricores. Weren't you paying attention to it on your leisure trip to Kenya?"

The Scotsman walked over to the doctor and gave him a hug that looked like it might break the old man in half. "You're the numpty that sent us on that wild goose chase, doctor!" he exclaimed. "The three of you look as clarty as squonks. Your trousers are manky. The lad tells me you were in the Underzoo. It's lucky you survived."

"Luck had nothing to do with it," said Cazador. "Jake and MIranda will tell you about it later. But when did you realize that Markus, Feng, and the others had betrayed us?"

Cormick frowned. "As ye know, doctor, I never trusted that

Bolo dunderheed. Sure enough, he must have been keeping an eye on us before we left, because he malafoostered our remote cameras."

"English, if you please, Cormick," said Cazador, smiling.

"Sorry. He broke 'em, didn't he? The professor kept texting us, telling us everything was perfit, but we knew something was wrong. It took us a while, but we hacked in remotely to one of the drones—those big 'uns we use for aerial mapping. Once we got the drone up and turned on its camera, we saw those black-shirted gits flooding in like rats, taking the animals out of their cages."

"We made an emergency landing in Morocco," continued Mrs. Equinox in her crisp British accent. "We refueled the plane and returned here as quickly as we could."

Marcelle handed Cazador his black walking staff. "We found this by the entrance to the Underzoo," she said. "So we had a suspicion of where you were. When we heard that Mrs. Jinks was looking for Jake and Miranda, we knew they must be with you."

"We had our hands full down there," said Cazador. "I never would have made it out of there without Jake and Miranda. They are full-fledged keepers now, by the way."

After the other keepers congratulated them, someone cleaned the doctor's wound and put a knee brace on his leg. Cormick brought Jake and Miranda sandwiches and soda. Dembi gave Pablo a sippy cup of black ink, which the little monkey glugged down.

"So do you already know about the trucks?" asked Jake as they ate. "It seems like all the cryptids are inside them."

"Aye, lad," said Cormick. "Most of 'em are anyway." He

turned to Cazador. "I hate to be the one to tell you, Cazador, but four trucks full of cryptids left before we got here. It was too late to follow 'em. They're gone, doctor."

Everyone on the hill grew quiet and looked at Cazador. His face darkened and a hardness appeared in his eyes. "Listen carefully," he said, his voice even and controlled. "This is what we're going to do."

Cazador described his plan to retake the zoo. As he spoke, Jake began to understand why this seemingly fragile, occasionally nutty, senior citizen had been able to capture the most dangerous creatures from around the world. It wasn't that he was a genius, though he might have been. His real gift was his utter *fearlessness*.

When he finished speaking, Cazador pushed himself up with his black staff. "You two stay with me," he told Miranda and Jake. "Diana says that your mother is with the police to the west of us. I'm in enough trouble with her already, so I don't want either of you taking any more risks. Understood?"

The sun was high in the cloudless sky as they descended the hillside. With Dembi in front, they made their way toward the trucks. When they reached level ground, he raised his right hand in a fist for them to stop. He continued on alone, slipping in behind the last truck. They watched as he cut the lock on the semi's doors before disappearing inside the trailer.

"We all know how fond of tatzelwurms you are, Jake," said Cazador, a mischievous gleam in his eye. "Do you think it will inject enough chaos into the situation if we let a few escape?"

Jake grinned. "I think that would probably work."

"Good," he said. "Because I told Dembi to let them *all* out."

Within a minute, the first tatzelwurm poked its ugly head

out of the truck's open back door. It arched its back and hissed, its spines growing rigid against its body. Soon, it was joined by eight others. Together they slithered off the tailgate and onto the ground, immediately making a beeline toward the guards. When the first man saw the pack of angry tatzelwurms coming toward them, he swore loudly and stumbled backwards. Once the other guards saw what was happening, they sprinted away from the animals toward the area where Cazador was hiding.

The doctor stepped out from the trees. "Drop your guns and get behind us. Otherwise, turn around and face the tatzelwurms."

The guards threw down their weapons as they ran past him into the woods. When the lizards saw Cazador and the rest of the team, they stopped. The lizard in front hissed. Then they turned and scuttled away.

"Secure the trucks!" yelled Cazador. "Quickly! There isn't much time. Markus will know we're here by now."

Miranda and Jake watched as the keepers opened up the front doors of the trucks, forcing the drivers out. Several bursts of gunfire erupted from the center of the compound.

Miranda grabbed Jake's arm. "Where's Mom?" she asked. "Do you think she's okay?"

"I'm sure she's fine," said Jake, though he was also worried. "She's probably sitting in a police car or something."

They followed Cazador toward the compound, leaving a few keepers behind to guard the trucks with the cryptids. "Last chance," he told them. "Could you both *please* stay here with the trucks?"

"Are you kidding?" said Jake. "We just won our first battle!

This is starting to get exciting."

Cazador shook his head and smiled. "You remind me of myself fifty years ago. Brave, foolish—"

A tremendous noise from the direction of the zoo cut him off. The three of them turned just in time to see the glass building on top of the tower disintegrate in a fiery explosion.

35

The Prince's Helicopter

Jake had seen plenty of explosions in his life—in the movies. In fact, if a film didn't have a terrorist plot, a high-speed car chase, or a kung-fu fight, his attention started to wander quickly.

It turns out that real-life explosions aren't nearly as much fun. Seconds after the glass building on the tower exploded, a gust of hot wind rushed past them, practically knocking them off their feet. Pablo, who sat perched atop Miranda's shoulder as usual, gave a high-pitched squeak and buried his head in her hair.

"Are you both all right?" asked the doctor.

"We're fine," replied Jake. "That was a little nuts. I hope nobody was in there."

"Are *you* okay, doctor?" asked Miranda. "I mean, your house that just blew up. And your office, too, I guess."

Cazador gazed at the flames on top of the tower, a faraway look in his eye. "To tell you the truth, I never really liked the place. Not much privacy, with all those windows. Sadly, most of my books and papers were in there." He frowned. "Let's end this nonsense before Markus blows up anything else."

They walked rapidly toward the chaotic scene now unfolding in the zoo compound. As they arrived at the first building, they found themselves in the middle of a battle between Becker's black-uniformed gunmen and the police. Cormick and Dembi took up positions behind the animal enclosures near the police officers. For almost five minutes the two sides exchanged gunfire. Soon the men in black seemed to realize they were outnumbered and began retreating toward the hills on the zoo's eastern border.

"Look at that!" exclaimed Jake. "They're running away. We're winning!"

"Perhaps," replied Cazador, scanning the area. "But we need to find Markus and Feng if we want to stop this for good. I want them to pay for what they've done."

"The men in those black uniforms are heading up the hill toward Elephant Ridge," said Miranda. "Maybe Professor Becker and Feng are waiting for them up there."

"I doubt it," Jake said. He glanced up at what remained of the glass building. It still burned like a torch, giving off a nasty chemical smell that made his eyes water. Flaming wreckage fell onto the roof of a nearby enclosure, which started to burn. "Knowing those two, they're staying as far away from the action as possible. Does the professor have an airplane?"

Cazador scratched his beard, thinking. "The zoo's landing strip is a mile north of here. But Cormick said that the police already took control of it, so that means no nearby airplanes. I suppose Markus or Alaweed could have a helicopter somewhere. But where?"

"They could hide it among some trees," offered Miranda. "But there aren't many trees near the main compound, except out on the island. There are plenty out there."

"That's it, *mi hija!*" shouted Cazador, pounding his staff on the ground. "*Vámonos!* Let's get a closer look at that island."

Cazador led them past the aviary and the squonk enclosure toward the aquarium. Black-clad mercenaries were being taken away in handcuffs by the Ranchita police. The sounds of gunfire were farther away now and not as frequent. Cormick, Dembi, and the others were pushing Professor Becker's men out of the valley.

When they reached Lake Lola, Jake saw a small beach area with a dock extending into the lake. One of the zoo's red motorboats was tied to the dock. A gentle breeze caused the boat to bob up and down in the water. They stared out at the island with its thick grove of pines. The island was as long a couple football fields. It resembled an aircraft carrier covered in trees.

"Are we too late?" asked Miranda. "I don't see anyone out there. Maybe they already left."

Cazador used a hand to shade his eyes against the sun. "I don't think so," he said. "Look more closely. Do you notice anything unusual?"

"It appears that some of the trees were recently knocked down," said Jake. "Over there, toward the end of the island."

"You're right," said Miranda excitedly. "It's as if someone carved out a space in the middle of the forest."

Cazador pulled out a small pair of binoculars from his battered suit jacket and handed them to Jake. "Tell us what you see, *mi hijo,*" he said.

Jake trained the binoculars on the island. He saw a dozen or so trees that had been cut down and piled to one side. Then he noticed a long, metallic blade jutting out from the tree line. He traced the blade to a black helicopter, barely visible among the trees. A short, overweight man in a fancy black suit stood next to the helicopter. He wore dark sunglasses and had a thick, black mustache. He gestured angrily at a tough-looking man holding a machine gun.

"There's a helicopter all right," said Jake, returning the binoculars to Cazador. "I saw two guys next to it. One of them had a rifle. They looks like they're waiting for something."

Cazador peered through the binoculars at the island. "For some*one*, I think," he remarked. "You saw that portly, well-dressed gentleman with the mustache?"

"I saw him," replied Jake. "He looks like a villain in a James Bond movie. He was yelling at the guy next to him."

"The yeller is Prince Alaweed," he said. "He's a vicious brute, but has more money and power than most governments. The man he's yelling at is his enforcer, Colonel Hassan. I'm shocked that Alaweed is here in person. This operation obviously means more to him than I realized. He must be quite irritated that Markus botched the takeover of the Z.I.A. Or maybe he doesn't understand yet that the game is up." He glanced at a small boathouse next to the dock. "But Markus knows. Don't you, Professor?"

Miranda and Jake looked from Cazador to the boathouse and then at each other.

Oh, no, thought Jake. Cazador is speaking to inanimate objects. The stress of the past few days has finally driven him crazy!

36

The Professor Takes a Swim

Before they could inform Cazador that no one was there, Professor Becker opened the boathouse door and walked onto the dock. He wore the same Z.I.A. uniform he'd had on when they last saw him, but it was now wrinkled and dirty. His blonde hair was disheveled and he hadn't shaved in days. In a few moments, Feng joined him.

The professor raised a pistol until it was level with their chests. "I gave Bolo two simple tasks," he said, his voice dripping with scorn. "Bring me the crypticon and make sure the three of you disappeared forever. He failed me on both counts. It's so difficult to find good help these days." He frowned, studying them. "How did you know where I was?"

Cazador put his arms around Jake and Miranda. "My newest keepers told me that you'd have a quick means of escape as soon as you saw your plans falling apart." He pointed to the boat. "Also, you left your overnight bag in the boat there. Your cowardice has made you sloppy and predictable, Markus."

"Cowardice!" exclaimed Becker in disgust. "It's called intelligence. While you were playing hide and seek with Bolo and his friends down in the Underzoo, I downloaded everything from your hard drives. The prince now has all the Z.I.A.'s deepest secrets, including the details of your upcoming unicorn expedition. I also managed to ship out a few dozen of your rarest cryptids before your keepers returned. I'd say this has been a fairly successful operation."

Cazador's eyes flashed with anger, but he didn't say anything.

"By the way," continued Becker. "You actually did me a favor by getting rid of Bolo. Now there's a bigger share of the profits for me." Feng shot him an annoyed look. "Relax, Alan. You'll get your cut, too."

Jake stepped forward. "You've lost, professor," he said. "We found the trucks with the cryptids. Look around you—we've taken back the zoo."

Miranda nodded. "And Dembi, Cormick, and about fifty cops will be here any minute," she added. "You should surrender while you can."

The professor sneered at them disdainfully. "Who cares if I didn't manage to steal Cazador's entire menagerie? When I find the unicorn, it will make up for everything. And once Alaweed and his engineers figure out how to make a crypticon using your files—"

"Excuse me, professor," interrupted Feng nervously. "We need to get out to the island right now. The prince says he's leaving in two minutes, with or without us."

Becker scowled at Cazador, tightening his grip on the pistol. His whole body radiated an intense hatred for the old man. "It's a pity I don't have more time," he snarled, as he walked toward the boat. "But I promise you someday I'll do what Bolo and all your monsters in the Underzoo failed to do—put you and the Z.I.A. out of commission permanently."

Professor Becker joined Feng in the boat and sat down in

the front seat. He turned the key in the ignition and the motor roared to life. Jake, Miranda, and Cazador looked on helplessly as the boat fishtailed across the water toward the island.

Cazador sighed. "I'm afraid this time Markus is right. Once he's safely inside one of Prince Alaweed's secret compounds, we'll never bring him to justice—or locate my missing cryptids."

Jake shook his head in disbelief. This is so unfair, he thought. After everything that happened, Becker was going to get away without a scratch. On the island, the blades of the helicopter started to rotate. Alaweed's men scurried about, loading equipment into the chopper. Behind him, Jake heard people shouting their names, but his eyes remained fixed on the motor boat skimming across the lake. In less than a minute, it would arrive at the island.

Then something happened that—even after all the bizarre, wonderful, frightening, jaw-dropping, and downright unbelievable things that had occurred during their summer at the Z.I.A.—should have been *impossible.*

Between the motorboat and the island, the lake seemed to boil and churn. Suddenly, it was like a submarine erupted out of the lake. But this was no submarine.

It was Lola—Cazador's long-lost sea serpent.

Jake couldn't believe his eyes. Lola was the *one* cryptid at the Z.I.A. he had been certain didn't exist. But the massive animal rising out of the water directly in front of the oncoming boat wasn't a figment of his imagination. Even though only half of Lola's body was visible above the water, she still made the boat look tiny. Her skin looked leathery and dark green, with small patches of black along her back. She had a gracefully arching neck at the end of which was an almost bird-like head with curious beach-ball-sized eyes the color of gold. She expelled water out of two large holes in her face that must have been nostrils.

"Welcome back, old girl," said Cazador, his voice shaky with emotion. "It's been a long time."

As soon as Professor Becker saw Lola, he swerved sharply to the left, barely avoiding a head-on collision with the animal's chest. The boat shuddered and then flipped, skipping across the water and flinging Feng and the professor directly in front of the animal. In a few seconds, another shape broke the surface of the water next to Lola. It was only half the size of the larger creature, but otherwise it was identical.

Miranda laughed and clapped her hands together. "It's a baby!" she exclaimed. "Lola was pregnant after all. Look, Cazador—you have a brand new baby sea serpent!"

The doctor smiled and shook his head. "Cormick was right all along," he said. "Now I'll never hear the end of it."

Lola's baby was as big as a full-grown elephant. It inclined its long neck downward until it was eye to eye with Becker and Feng, who sputtered and thrashed about in the water. When the two men finally noticed Lola's baby inspecting them, they screamed and began swimming frantically toward shore.

The baby sea serpent recoiled and gave a high-pitched cry. Immediately mindful of her child's distress, Lola let loose with a tremendous snort of her nose as loud as the horn of a cruise liner. Together, the two animals dived into the water, sending a mini-tidal wave that snatched up the two hapless men and sent them tumbling toward shore.

Then the sea serpents were gone, leaving behind them only

waves that caused the dock to tilt wildly against the shore.

"I can't believe Lola existed this whole time," said Jake, staring out at the water. "I've been swimming in that lake! I'm lucky I wasn't eaten."

"I think Lola prefers the arapaima," said Cazador. "Besides, haven't I always told both of you the truth?" He paused. "I mean, *eventually.*"

Miranda smiled. "Yes, you have, doctor," she said. "So I guess I won't give up my dream of finding a unicorn."

"I should think not!" the doctor exclaimed. "In fact, that unicorn expedition is now my highest priority. I can't allow Prince Alaweed to capture the most famous cryptid in the world before I do."

As Becker and Feng continued to struggle to shore, two black helicopters rose up from the island. They banked over the lake before turning south. In less than a minute, they disappeared behind the distant mountains. At that moment, a crowd of people from the Z.I.A. marched down the hill toward the lake.

"Look, Jake, here comes Mom," exclaimed Miranda. "I've never been happier to see anybody in my life!"

Suddenly, Pablo left Miranda and climbed up Jake's leg onto his shoulder. "Oh, so *now* you want to hang out with me," said Jake. "Better late than never, I guess."

Maybe he *was* an animal lover after all, he thought as he scratched Pablo's chin. Or maybe he just liked the ones weird enough to be called cryptids.

Miranda grinned and glanced at Cazador. "You know, doctor, we still have a few more weeks of summer. I bet we could help you plan your unicorn hunt. After all, you *did* make us full-fledged keepers."

"She's right," added Jake quickly. "And how hard could it be to capture a semi-mythical horse with an ivory horn in the middle of its forehead? Piece of cake."

Cazador tugged at his beard thoughtfully. "Given everything that's happened over the past week," he said at last. "Convincing your mother to allow you to accompany me on a cryptid hunt around the world is quite simply an *impossible* task." He smiled. "Luckily, the impossible happens to be my specialty."

END OF BOOK ONE

Robert Crisell is a writer, actor, and attorney, though he prefers to think of himself as a full-time Shakespearean. His first job after college was assistant editor at *Highlights for Children* magazine where he relearned the importance of jokes, riddles, and a good story. He lives in California with his wife, two children, and the occasional tarantula. This is his first novel.

WWW.ROBCRISELL.COM